THE MUMMY'S TOMB

Also by ROY POND:

The Mummy's Revenge

THE MUMMY'S TOMB

Original title:
The Mummy Tomb Hunt

ROY POND

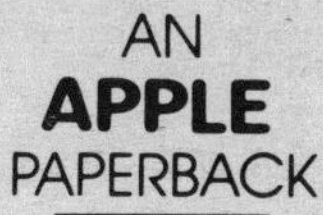

SCHOLASTIC INC.
New York Toronto London Auckland Sydney

ISBN 0-590-60370-1

 Published by Scholastic Inc., 555 Broadway, New York, NY 10012, by arrangement with Omnibus Books. APPLE PAPERBACKS and the APPLE logo are registered trademarks of Scholastic Inc.

12 11 10 9 8 7 6 5 4 3 2 1 6 7 8 9/9 0 1/0

Printed in the U.S.A. 40

First Scholastic printing, March 1996

Contents

For Quest and Lorelei

The Mummy's Tomb

Mediterranean Sea
EGYPT
CAIRO
N
The flight
to join the
cruise boat
River Nile
Red Sea
ABYDOS
LUXOR
ESNA
EDFU
KOM OMBO
ASWAN
PHILAE
The cruise
of the
Tutankhamun
starts here
ABU SIMBEL
THE
CRUISE
ON THE
NILE

1

The Little Games Shop in Cairo

Harry pressed his nose to the window. Behind the misted glass he could see what looked like an ancient Egyptian god with broad shoulders and an animal head.

"I told you this shop was creepy," he said.

Harry, and his older cousins Josh and Amy, were outside a little shop called Magical Isis Games and Novelties, at the bottom of a dim arcade in Cairo. The window was crowded with decals of Egyptian gods and goddesses, hieroglyphic symbols, and signs in Arabic and English. There was barely a clear spot of window to see through, Josh thought, especially with Harry taking up so much room and steaming up the glass.

The figure in the window stood as if taking a step forward. One arm was held stiffly against its side and the other was raised above its head, as though it was about to strike a blow or call down a bolt of lightning from the heavens. The animal head had square-tipped, upraised ears and an ant-eater snout that seemed to be hooked in a permanent snarl.

The creature was a game model, cast in metal in the

form of the Egyptian god Seth. Beneath it the three children discovered an army of miniatures with the heads of jackals, falcons, beetles, snakes, cats and crocodiles. Displayed beyond these weird-looking models were boxes of puzzles, role-playing games, jigsaws of the pyramids and temples of Karnak and Luxor, and computer games with an Egyptian theme.

Josh was lured by the computer games, even though he tried to resist them. He was trying to forget about them after his experience with the terrifying Mummy Monster Game, which the three of them had played together not long ago, back home.

"What's that?" Amy said. "Look over there."

"I'm trying to," Josh said irritably. "But Harry's stuck against the window like a squashed fly. Give us a look at the games, Harry."

"Not the games," Amy said. "Look at the people inside the shop. Are they alive?"

Harry removed his face from the window. "It must be the owner, Mr Aboudy, and his son."

The shop was dark inside, but a computer screen on the counter threw bands of coloured light across the forms of a man and a boy slumped on stools. They weren't sitting up at the counter but were flopped over it, arms dangling, cheeks resting flat on the counter top, eyes closed in peaceful repose. It was as if they had fallen down dead.

"They're having a siesta," Harry explained. "The Egyptians try to grab a nap around this time of the day."

Josh and Amy had wondered why the area seemed so deserted. Yesterday, when they visited the pyramids and the sphinx, Cairo had been crowded with people, and the streets were full of honking traffic; and it had been just the same earlier that morning on their short trip to the museum to see the famous golden treasures of Tutankhamun. They had gone there with Harry's mother, their Aunt Jillian, who was an Egyptologist. Aunt Jillian had stayed on at the museum for a meeting with the Antiquities authorities, and Harry had brought his cousins here into this shopping arcade. It was not far from the Rameses Hilton hotel, where they were staying before boarding a cruise boat for a cruise down the Nile.

"Funny. That's not the Aboudys," Harry said. "I wonder where they are? Let's go inside."

Amy stopped him. "But we can't."

"Why not?"

"We can't wake them up."

"Of course we can. The shop's open."

"They might be upset."

"They'd be more upset if they missed a sale."

"How can you have the heart to wake them? They're sleeping so peacefully."

Harry grinned. "Maybe they're having bad dreams and they'll be glad we woke them. I'm going in."

He opened the door, which set off a bell in the shop. Josh and Amy followed him inside.

The man and the boy shot up from the counter as if someone had pressed a lever. In one comical movement they were both on their feet, sweeping away their stools and producing dustcloths which they used to wipe away the smudges on the counter top. They looked as if they'd been busy for hours.

"*Naharak sa'eed*," Harry said. "That means good day," he whispered to the others.

"Welcome," the man said in a deep, educated voice.

He had raised himself to an impressive height, a bony-faced man dressed in a striped galabea gown. His eyes, though reddened with sleep, were instantly watchful.

The boy, who was not much bigger than Harry, wore a blue galabea and had big, dreamy eyes, like those of a statue they had seen in the Cairo museum of the young prince Tutankhamun.

"I hope we didn't interrupt any pleasant dreams," Amy said apologetically.

"We were dreaming that you would come into our shop," the man said. If it was meant as a joke, he wasn't smiling.

"Where's Mr Aboudy and his son?" Harry asked. "I always buy games from this shop when I visit Cairo."

Wariness drew a blind across the man's eyes.

"Mr Aboudy is away. We are temporary staff. He will be back soon, *Inshalla*."

"Inshalla means 'if god is willing'," Harry translated for the others in an undertone. "Egyptians say it after every statement about the future." He returned his attention to the shop attendant. "I bought the Mummy Monster Game here," he told him.

The man nodded. "A most challenging game," he said.

"Not for us. We cracked it," Harry said. He looked at the Egyptian boy. If he expected to see any flicker of admiration in response, he was disappointed. The boy's eyes flashed resentfully.

"You think you are clever," the boy said.

"Pretty good."

"What you want?"

"Another game," Harry said. "Something for my portable game gear. We're going on a Nile cruise and I want something we can play along the way."

"You think you can find the mummy's secret?"

"That sounds good," Harry said. "The Mummy's Secret Game?"

"There is no game called the Mummy's Secret Game."

"But you said ..."

"I did not."

Harry was getting rattled. "I like Mr Aboudy's son better," he whispered to Josh and Amy. "He's friendly."

"Allow me, sir," the man said. "I have just the game for you."

As he bent to unlock a door under the counter, Josh noticed his long, hooked nose. Where had he seen a nose like that recently? He remembered. It was the statue of Seth in the window of the shop.

"Where are you going on your cruise?" the man asked.

"We're going to Aswan first," Harry said. "While we're there we visit the temple of Abu Simbel in the desert and the island temple of Philae, then we start cruising downstream, stopping at Kom Ombo, Edfu, Esna and Luxor, before going on to Abydos. Then we pop back to Luxor for our return flight to Cairo."

The man searched under the counter for a while, then he brought out a brightly coloured box. On the cover was the title THE MUMMY TOMB HUNT. Beneath it was an illustration of an Egyptian god—or a man—with a black jackal head. The figure was bending over a mummy stretched out on a funerary couch.

"Wow! What do we have to do?"

"Play the game," the boy said.

"I know that. But how?"

"You think you are clever. You work it out."

"No, I mean what's the game about?"

"A tomb."

"Whose tomb?"

"Allow me," the man said. "The Mummy Tomb Hunt is a hunt for the lost tomb of a forgotten pharaoh. It will set you riddles to solve and clues to find in the tombs and temples you will visit. Some clues are important; others are not. Some, if you can decipher their meaning, may help you find the pharaoh's tomb."

"An adventure quest game—they're the best! What do we find at the end?"

"A surprise," the Egyptian boy said with an unpleasant smile.

"Be warned," the man said. "The Mummy Tomb Hunt is not easy. There are difficult puzzles, dangerous tomb traps ... if you get that far."

Josh wanted to pick up the box and read the back, but stopped himself.

"What do you think, Josh?"

Josh shrugged. "I haven't time for computer games."

"But we'll have almost a week on the cruise."

"He's been a bit scared off by computer games," Amy

explained, looking at her brother sympathetically.

"You haven't stopped playing games, have you, Josh?" Harry said in a concerned voice.

The two behind the counter turned their eyes on Josh.

Josh frowned. Why am I suddenly the centre of attention? he thought. Harry's doing the shopping.

"He was frightened by the monster that lurks within," the man said, as if he knew it to be a fact.

What monster? What did he mean? Did he mean the monster within the game, or within himself?

"I'm not so hooked on games any more, that's all," Josh said. But he couldn't help looking at the picture of the jackal-headed figure on the cover of the Mummy Tomb Hunt. The pointy ears and snout promised a game full of challenges and wily tricks.

"This one will take hold of you," the man assured him.

Harry turned to Amy. "What do you think, Amy?"

"It's up to you, Harry, but I don't think you should waste your holiday playing computer games."

"It wouldn't be wasting my holiday to look for a lost pharaoh's tomb."

"But that's in the game, Harry. It'd be much more fun looking for a *real* lost pharaoh's tomb."

"Perhaps, just perhaps," the man said in a guarded voice, "this game might lead you to one." He exchanged a glance with the Egyptian boy.

"I'll take it," Harry said.

"Don't you want to haggle?" Amy whispered. "My guide book says you are expected to haggle before you buy."

"I'm not haggling for this," Harry said. "It sounds

brilliant. Just what I've been saving all my pocket money for! We're going to have a great time with this game."

"*Inshallah*," the man intoned in his deep voice.

If god is willing.

2

A Flight of Fantasy

"Harry's a worse gamehead than you used to be, Josh," Amy said, shaking her head.

They were flying from Cairo to the far south of Egypt and would soon be arriving at Aswan, the starting point for their cruise down the Nile—yet here was Harry already taking out his hand-held computer game gear.

Harry slid the new game cartridge into the back of the machine and switched on the battery power. The little red eye of the power light came on. He angled the console enticingly towards them so that Josh and Amy could see.

The small, high-resolution, back-lit LCD screen flickered and then came glowingly to life. The name SETH SOFTWARE TM slid up in red letters, and a chorus of shimmery female voices chanted "The Mummy Tomb Hunt". A title screen appeared. Like the cover, it showed a full-colour graphic of an Egyptian god or priest with a jackal head, bending over a mummy on a funerary couch. Music, an adventure theme with a driving beat, blipped out of the speaker. The words *Press start button* flashed on to the screen.

Harry turned and grinned at his cousins before jabbing the blue start button with his thumb.

"Do you want to play, Josh?"

"No thanks."

"Amy?"

"No thanks, Harry."

Harry never knew when to stop with games, Josh thought, scowling at him. Games were trouble. A game had almost swallowed him up once. Never again. He shuddered.

He remembered every single detail of the Mummy Monster Game. They had played it in the darkness of his bedroom at home when Harry had been staying with them. It hadn't been a hand-held game like this one. He pictured the big screen filled with the image of a tomb passage. The glowing lines of the passage, converging in infinity, had pulsed and hummed and drawn first their eyes and then their senses to the centre of the screen. Still in the bedroom, they had felt the temperature change and the press of cold stone surrounding them. Then the game had drawn them into a frightening quest to gather together the dismembered mummy parts of King Osiris, which had been scattered by his evil brother Seth. Each piece of Osiris—head, feet, arms, legs, heart—had been guarded by an Egyptian creature which had set the children fearsome challenges and riddles to solve.

Josh's drive to prove himself the best of the three players had brought them all to the edge of disaster. Amy, who did not like computer games, and Harry, who pretended to be afraid of nothing, had both become lost in the game. Finally Josh had found his courage and dared to revisit the Egyptian underworld alone to save the others. The experience had left him badly shaken.

Now Josh made himself look away from Harry's game. He tried to ignore the music, which pulled at him like a thread. If he followed it, he knew that it would lead him back into the maze of lost time, lost feelings, lost living and a loss of caring about anyone else in the world.

Don't listen to it. Close your ears. Listen to the hum of the jet engines.

Josh moved as far away from the game as he could, and pressed his face against the window. Looking down, far below, he saw a town in Upper Egypt bathed in afternoon sunlight.

They were about to enjoy an exciting holiday with Aunt Jillian and Harry on board the Nile cruiser *Tutankhamun*. Their aunt had originally planned to take only Harry with her, but at the last moment there had been cancellations by other passengers and some spare cabins had become available. She had hit on the wonderful idea of inviting Josh and Amy to join them.

Josh and Amy's mother had been only too happy to have them occupied for the school holidays, and she had offered to pay for their air fares. It had all happened so suddenly that Josh could scarcely believe that they were actually here, flying over the land of Egypt.

Outside the window he could see the sweep of the aeroplane wing and, slung beneath it, the bulge of a jet engine pod. Painted on the engine pod in red, gold and black was the symbol of the airline Egyptair: the mask-like profile of a falcon, the ancient Egyptian god Horus, son of Osiris.

As the music from Harry's game tugged at him, it seemed to Josh that the black eye of the falcon emblem swivelled in its socket to fix on him accusingly.

Josh pulled his head back so quickly he banged his ear on the rim of the window. He couldn't have been more startled if he'd seen flames wrap around the engine. *The eye in the falcon's head had appeared to move.* He looked at Amy to see if she'd noticed, but her head was bent over a book. Harry was wrestling with the game gear, his tongue protruding from the corner of his mouth. Josh swallowed hard, then shook his head as if to shake the silly idea out of his mind, like a diver shaking water out of his ears after a dive. Cautiously he put his face back to the glass.

The sound of Harry's game seemed to grow louder.

Maybe a shred of passing cloud had whipped past the painted eye and created the illusion. Harry's game was making him jumpy, bringing back memories of that other game and that other time he would rather forget.

"Isn't it great, Josh?" Amy said. "School holidays—and we're thousands of kilometres away from home!" His sister had two books balanced on her knees. One was a guide book to Egypt's archaeological sites, the other a small travel diary.

"What?"

"We're really in Egypt! Not just in a game."

"Don't talk to me about games!"

"That's all you used to talk about once, remember."

"Well, maybe I'm growing out of them."

"I'm glad, Josh. There's more to life than games."

"Tell that to Harry. I don't think he could care less about being here," Josh said. "Maybe he's been to Egypt too many times."

Harry hadn't bothered to glance out of the window once. He might as well have been lounging in a chair at home for all the excitement he showed. He was more interested in the game.

The game *did* look interesting, though, Josh had to admit. Like Harry, he thought adventure quest games were the best of all. He loved the idea of finding treasure.

Amy craned her neck to look over Harry's shoulder at the console's small colour screen, and obligingly he turned it again to give her a better view. The colour graphics on the screen grabbed Josh's attention. They showed a map of Egypt, with the blue-green River Nile running through a narrow band of cultivation bordered by desert. The map was blank, with no names on it.

Instructions appeared on the screen: *Find answers to the riddles you will be given, and more details will appear on this map. Your quest begins at the first archaeological site you visit.*

Josh was intrigued. How could the game know which archaeological site they would be visiting first? Or was it so general that it would apply to any site?

The screen now changed to a play sequence. It was the usual sort of platform game that Josh was used to seeing on portable game consoles. A cartoon figure in the khaki field clothes of an archaeologist was racing for his life through a length of stone passageway in a maze, pursued by a stone pharaoh with a sword. The passage branched suddenly like a fork of lightning and Harry tried to switch his character's direction with a flick of the direction button. Too slow. The archaeologist missed the turning and ran on, still pursued by the pharaoh.

I would have made that turn, Josh thought. I'm still better than Harry. Those young fingers aren't sharp enough.

Now the archaeologist rushed up to a pit filled with crocodiles. Josh felt his fingers twitch and shape themselves around an imaginary console in his hands. His thumb went for the jump button. *Quick, Harry!* The old game-player sat up inside Josh, wanting to take over. Harry stabbed the button and his character leaped over the gap and landed safely on the other side. *Good.*

Good?

What am I thinking? I don't care about that stuff, Josh thought, relaxing his fingers. It's just a dumb game.

Yet he would have enjoyed playing it once—before he'd come to believe that his obsession with computer games was dangerous. His mother had told him so often enough, and so had Amy. The Mummy Monster Game had shown him what happened when you put this obsession ahead of everything else, especially ahead of other people.

He had given up playing, but now there was a gap in his life.

There's more to life than computer games, Amy had said.

Yes, but what?

He glanced at his ponytailed sister, who had gone back

to reading her guide book. Amy was always studying something, filling her mind with facts. His glance moved on, past Harry and across the aisle to where Aunt Jillian sat. She was reading from a sheaf of typed notes, a pair of owlish reading glasses perched on the end of her nose. In between her archaeological excavations, she was to give a series of lectures to the cruise passengers, and she was preparing some notes for her talks.

Josh wondered what secrets she would have to tell.

3

The Cruise Begins

It was dusk by the time they reached their destination.

The Nile cruiser *Tutankhamun* lay berthed at the quay at Aswan. Josh felt a stir of excitement at the sight of it. Aglow with lights, it was a golden cruise boat with a three-storey superstructure and accommodation for sixty passengers. Its bow and stern curved up sheerly from the water in the ancient Egyptian style, ending in golden posts with heads that flared like papyrus plants.

They went up a gangway, through an entrance with a carved pylon like that leading into an Egyptian temple, and into the boat. Inside, it was like walking into the reception of a modern hotel. They were shown to their cabins by a smiling steward wearing a blue jacket. All the decks had different names. Their cabins were on Sobek Deck.

"Sobek was the ancient Egyptian crocodile god," Aunt Jillian told them. "I suppose it's appropriate seeing we're on the lower deck—closest to the river."

Josh and Harry were given one cabin to share, and Amy and Aunt Jillian shared another next door. Josh looked around their cabin in delight. As big as a hotel room, it had two beds, a wardrobe and dresser, chairs, a picture window and its own bathroom.

Aunt Jillian took them out onto the deck.

She breathed in the warm evening air, sighing with pleasure as if she had just come home after a long absence. Stars were coming out in a sky that was beginning to turn midnight blue, and the lights of the small town of Aswan sparkled on the water.

Aunt Jillian pointed to the far side of the river. "See those cliffs over there?" They followed her line of direction. Across the river, caramel-coloured floodlit cliffs rose like a fortress, with a long sweep of stone steps leading to the top.

"If you look hard you'll see a small row of dark rectangles high up in the cliff," she said in her soft voice. "Can you guess what they are?" Aunt Jillian always spoke quietly, as if she were sharing a secret with the children. It made them listen hard to what she said.

"They're tombs," Harry said.

"Not you, Harry," she chided him. "I'm asking Josh and Amy. Give them a chance! You've been here before."

"They're the Tombs of the Nomarchs," Amy said, surprising them all.

"And who were the Nomarchs?"

"Local governors who ruled in the pharaoh's name."

"Quite right!" said Aunt Jillian. "The Nomarchs used to rule here for the pharaohs who lived in faraway Thebes and Memphis." She smiled at Amy approvingly. "You've been swotting up, Amy. I noticed you hard at work on the plane."

Amy beamed. "I enjoy studying."

"Yes, even on holidays," Josh grumbled. "She's never out of school. Amy's always knocking herself out."

"Just because you won't pick up a book, Josh, is no reason to criticise other people," Amy said.

"Well, there's a time for studying and there's a time for enjoyment," Aunt Jillian told them. "And knowledge is not nearly so important as what you make of it, what conclusions you draw from it, what you feel about it. I hope you children are going to relax and steep yourselves in Egypt. Enjoy yourselves. You're on holiday on the most fabulous river on earth."

"Good, you tell them, Mum," Harry said. "Neither of them would play my new computer game with me."

"Wouldn't they now?"

"I'm sure your mother doesn't approve of computer games," Amy said to Harry, expecting support from her aunt. "Mine doesn't. She thinks they are a waste of time."

Aunt Jillian looked at Josh. "I heard that you were mad about computer games, Josh."

Josh wondered what to say. Like most adults, Aunt Jillian probably had a low opinion of computer games.

"Well ..."

"Josh is fantastic at games," Harry put in. "You should have seen the way he played the Mummy Monster Game. We would all have been lost without him. Amy was pretty good too, although she wouldn't admit it."

Amy made a small, strangled sound as she remembered the game and the nightmares it had put them through.

"I don't think being good at anything is ever a waste," Aunt Jillian said to Josh. "I believe we are given skills for a reason—and as long as we use those skills in a good cause, that's all that matters. Being good at games actually means you have valuable problem-solving skills. Keep those skills sharp, Josh. One day they'll serve you well."

Josh couldn't believe his ears. Neither could Amy. She frowned at Aunt Jillian in puzzlement.

"Don't you think games can be bad?"

"Bad in what sense?"

"Scary. Some of Harry's Egyptian games are pretty scary."

"I don't find Egypt scary. The Egyptians weren't dismal people obsessed with death and curses. They loved life. They loved life so much that they wanted it to go on. That's why they built their tombs and had their bodies preserved by mummification, thinking it would guarantee them an existence after death. Wait till you go into the tombs. They aren't at all gloomy. The royal tombs are vibrant places, and the reliefs and paintings are full of lively detail and are quite beautiful."

Josh felt himself warming to Aunt Jillian. She was the first adult he'd ever met who valued something he was good at. He felt drawn to this aunt who had spent so much of her life away from home, on excavations in Egypt. He'd always wanted to know more about her. Maybe he was going to enjoy this time with her.

He was already impressed by Egypt. This was their first stroll on the deck and already they'd spotted tombs. He focused on one of the small doorways in the cliff and wondered what it would be like to go inside it—into a real Egyptian tomb.

"Are there tombs everywhere?" he asked.

"Just about. Tombs are never very far away in Egypt. They open everywhere, like doorways to eternity. Especially on the western side of the Nile. That was considered to be the Land of the Dead, because that's where the sun died each day."

"I've been up to the top of that cliff," Harry said. "It's not much fun climbing all those stone steps. My legs were wobbly as jelly when I got to the top, and a sandstorm came along before we got down and blew sand in our eyes."

"Are we going there?" Amy said. She sounded as though she had lost some of her enthusiasm for the Tombs of the Nomarchs.

"No, we'll be seeing some far grander tombs later, in the Valley of the Kings and the Valley of the Queens."

"Have you ever dug up a pharaoh's treasure?" Josh asked.

"Egyptologists don't really dig for treasure. They dig for facts. However, I have been on the track of one particular treasure for years. Somewhere, I know, there's an intact undiscovered tomb of a forgotten pharaoh."

Forgotten pharaoh? Interesting, Josh thought. The man in the games shop had also mentioned a forgotten pharaoh's tomb.

"What was it that hooked you on Egyptology?" Amy asked her aunt. "Was it the mystery and romance of Egypt?"

"I became an Egyptologist because I hated mystery. I hated not knowing things." One of the things they were learning about Aunt Jillian was that she never reacted in the way they expected. "When I was a child, my parents took me to the mummy room of the British Museum. I walked around in a daze staring at all those bodies wrapped in their dusty old bandages. I couldn't understand it. Why did they do it? I went on to other exhibits and my mystification grew. It seemed that the Egyptians had a special hold on eternity, and it wasn't just in their mummies. Even their statues seemed to stare down the centuries with a look of calm assurance. And then I learned about the pyramids, the oldest wonders of the world. That's when I decided that I had to find out everything there was to know about these people. So you see, it's not just what attracts us that is significant, but what disturbs us, too. Often it's more revealing, and it's the real clue to what we should pursue in our lives."

"Have you found out all the mysteries now?"

Aunt Jillian made a rueful face. "No—particularly since I've never found that intact tomb I've been searching for. It's a dream all archaeologists have. But big finds are rare. We do most of our work with a brush and a sieve rather than a pick and shovel. It's a painstaking job, and backbreaking, too, but you keep on going."

"Tell us about this tomb you've been searching for," Josh said, his interest deepening.

"I'll be talking about it in a lecture I'm giving in the passenger lounge before dinner. I've got colour slides to show. You'll come along, won't you?" She looked at her wristwatch. "In fact, I'd better go and set up the slide projector."

"We'll skip the lecture," Harry whispered, when she

had gone. "I've been to dozens of Mum's talks."

"But *we* haven't, Harry," Amy said.

"I don't want to miss it," Josh said firmly.

Amy looked at her brother in surprise.

Harry gave in. "All right," he said. "But it hasn't started yet, so let's go and explore."

On the upper deck of the *Tutankhamun* there was an area under canvas as well as an open space with deck-chairs around a small swimming pool.

"That's for me!" said Amy.

"And me," said Josh.

"And me," said Harry.

Beyond the pool was the passenger lounge, where Aunt Jillian was setting up her slide projector.

They went down the steps of a companionway to the next level to discover a hairdressing salon and a shop stocked with clothes, toiletries and gifts. The next deck contained the reception area, while the lower deck held the restaurant, a medical clinic and a room crammed with well-filled bookcases.

"A library!" Amy said delightedly. "That's for me!"

"Not for me," said Harry.

"Nor for me," said Josh.

And this time Amy did not look surprised.

4

The Forgotten Pharaoh

The projector whirred, the slide carousel turned, and another slide dropped down into the gate.

A scene of a desolate valley surrounded by cliffs was beamed on to the screen at the front of the crowded passenger lounge. Beside it stood Aunt Jillian with the remote control unit in her hand. She was in the middle of her first lecture.

Josh tried to focus his attention. He wanted to hear this. He could not shake out of his mind what his aunt had said about a forgotten pharaoh.

Aunt Jillian pointed to the screen.

"This is the valley where I made what I thought would be my biggest find. I had been on the track of this tomb for years. It's the tomb of a pharaoh who does not appear on the king lists, at least not in the period in which he lived. His name is Heri-hor. Here is the tomb."

She pushed the button and the scene changed to show a close-up of a tomb entrance. The dark wedge of the doorway looked mysterious and disquieting.

Josh sat forward in his chair.

"Before I take you inside the tomb, I'd like to go back a bit and show you one of the steps that led to finding it. My search began with the discovery of this humble tomb here."

Another image filled the screen. It was a photograph taken inside a tomb, showing a small barrel-vaulted chamber cut out of the rock. "This was the tomb of a royal architect named Setekhy." More slides followed, showing paintings and carvings on the wall. The audience saw Setekhy seated with his wife under vines, in a garden beside an ornamental pool. Under his wife's chair a cat was playing. Another carved relief showed some boatmen jousting on the river. They were standing on narrow papyrus skiffs and were lunging at each other with long poles, trying to push each other into the river. Beneath the surface of the water lurked a crocodile, waiting to seize the loser.

"A fine tomb, but modest compared with the tomb I was seeking," Aunt Jillian told her audience. "What intrigued me was this niche, because inscribed in this niche is a boast." She changed the slide to show some hieroglyphics. "I'll read it to you: *I, Setekhy, architect and minister of his majesty Heri-hor, did cause to furnish the royal tomb in the valley, none other seeing and none other knowing.*"

She changed the slide again.

"This alerted me to the existence of another royal tomb in the valley, and after patient detective work I eventually found the tomb of this pharaoh Heri-hor. But before I did that, I also came upon these mysterious words inscribed in the tomb of Setekhy:

"And the dead king, the Osiris Heri-hor, flew like a bird to be reunited with the sun god in his heavenly Boat of Millions of Years. I supervised the pilgrimage journey of his coffin to Abydos so that he could visit the Staircase of the God Osiris—the ladder to heaven—before returning for his burial in the great Seat of Silence of his forefathers. This I did like a high priest leaving the shrine of a god, walking out backwards and wiping the ground with palm leaves to hide my footsteps."

Another slide appeared on the screen. "I'll now take you inside the tomb of the pharaoh."

Aunt Jillian took her audience through beautifully painted corridors decorated with scenes of feasting, fishing and hunting and the king making offerings. Finally, a slide revealed the burial chamber. Its pillars and walls were carved and painted, but the chamber itself was empty.

"This chamber is decorated with scenes from the Book of the Dead," Aunt Jillian said, "as well as a scene of the king's mummified body being taken by boat on a pilgrimage to the holy city of Abydos before its return to the Valley of the Kings and burial." She showed a painting of a funerary barque, its stem and stern upswept and the sarcophagus of the pharaoh lying on the deck.

Suddenly she switched off the projector and turned on the lights.

"Now, you may be wondering where the contents of this tomb are, and you may even imagine that they are lying in display cases inside some museum, but what you saw in this tomb is exactly what greeted my eyes when I opened it. Nothing. An intact, sealed tomb—and yet there was nothing inside. No mummy. No rich furnishings. Just a mystery.

"Mystery, ladies and gentlemen. That's one of the things I hate and love about archaeology. Thank you," Aunt Jillian finished.

The audience clapped.

They ate dinner in the crowded dining-room at the same table as the cruise director, the captain and two Egyptian guides.

Over dessert, Amy leaned over to her aunt and said, "I enjoyed your talk, Aunt Jillian. But don't you find it scary crawling around in tombs? And what about mummies? Aren't you scared of finding them?"

"No. I've found plenty of them. In fact, I've slept in tombs, in the same chamber as mummies. They can't harm you, Amy."

Amy looked at Aunt Jillian with a mixture of admiration and uneasiness, and shivered. "I couldn't sleep in the same room as a mummy."

"No? Well, I hope you can sleep in the same cabin as an aunt, because I'm pooped. We've got a big day tomorrow, all of us, so what about grabbing some sleep?"

They left the dining-room together and went along the passageway to their cabins.

"Tomorrow we visit two important sites in one day," Aunt Jillian told them. "In the morning we travel across the Aswan Dam to see the island temple of Philae, and in the afternoon we make a short flight to Abu Simbel to see the giant statues in the desert. I hope you packed some torches, by the way. I did mention it to your mother. It's a good thing to bring a torch with you to the tombs and temples. It can be very dark inside, even where they have lights, and you'll miss the beautiful reliefs and paintings."

"We've brought ours," Amy said.

"Good." She gave Amy and Josh one of her bright smiles and took Amy with her to their cabin.

"'Night," Josh said, going into his cabin with Harry.

When they were tucked up in their beds for the night, Harry switched on his computer game and started to play the Mummy Tomb Hunt.

Josh lay and listened to the music that filled their cabin. It had changed, he noted; it no longer suggested a chase, but rather a mysterious quest. Perhaps Aunt Jillian was right, he thought. Perhaps being good at computer games did prove something, and he didn't have to stop playing them, after all. It would be fun to play the Mummy Tomb Hunt with Harry.

"Wow!" Harry said.

Josh sat up. "What's happening?"

"We've got the first clues. One's about the island of Philae. The other's about Abu Simbel." He frowned. "That's a bit weird. We're going to visit both of those places tomorrow. But how could the game know?"

"Coincidence?"

"You think so?"

"Maybe all the cruises go to the same stops."

"They do, more or less. But they don't all start at Aswan and go downstream to Luxor and then Abydos.

Some go the other way."

Josh remembered something. "You told the man in the shop that we were sailing from Aswan," he reminded his cousin. "Maybe there are several versions of the game and he gave you the one that fitted our cruise."

"Maybe. Strange, though."

"What's the clue?"

Harry read from the screen:

"In Philae there's a place
where the priests have left no trace,
no footprints on the floor,
no divinity to adore.

"What do you reckon it means?" he asked.

"Perhaps it means nothing," replied Josh. "The man in the shop said some clues were important and others weren't. It could be a red herring—a clue that's drawn across the trail just to lead you off the scent and confuse you. What's the Abu Simbel clue?"

"I'll read it out," Harry said.

"Rameses multiplied himself
in search of lasting fame.
He fashioned four giant statues
his glory to proclaim.
He had a hundred sons and daughters
to further his proud aim,
but it is his hollow heart
that best repeats his name,

not once, not twice, not four times,
but again and again and again ..."

"We'd better write those riddles down," Josh said. He opened a drawer in his bedside table, scratched around, and found a pen and some laundry lists. He scribbled both riddles on the back of one of these and put it on the table for the morning. Then he yawned.

"Let's sleep on it," he said to Harry, reaching to switch off his lamp. "I'm tired."

"Okay," Harry said. "We can't do any more now, anyway. Don't let's forget to tell Amy about it in the morning."

Josh lay in bed, hugging to himself the knowledge that he was aboard a boat on the most famous river in history, a river that had carried ancient pharaohs and queens. Hatshepsut. Thutmosis. Akhenaten. Nefertiti. Tutankhamun. Rameses. Cleopatra.

It would be brilliant to find a *real* lost pharaoh's tomb ... but it would take more than Harry's Egyptian computer game to find one ... or would it?

You never knew with Harry and his weird games, he thought, before he drifted off to sleep.

5

The Riddle of Isis

"What are you looking at, Harry?" Aunt Jillian asked.

"Just a note," he replied evasively.

Harry was re-reading the two riddles Josh had recorded on the back of the laundry list.

They were in a puttering motorboat, travelling in a flotilla with other cruise passengers across the Aswan Dam. The boats were shaded by canopies from the brilliant morning sunshine.

Ahead of them, temple buildings and columns of stone rose into the sky from the lush greenery that fringed the island of Philae.

Aunt Jillian raised her voice above the noise of the outboard engine to tell them about the island. "This is not the real island of Philae," she explained. "When they built the Aswan Dam, the real island of ancient times began to sink beneath the waters. So a new site was chosen on the nearby island of Agilqiyyah, which was higher. The island you can now see was carved into exactly the same shape as the old island, and the entire temple was moved stone by stone."

It must have taken giants to move it, Josh thought, looking at the soaring temple.

Amy held out her hand to Harry and he passed her the note. They had told her about the clues at breakfast, but she wanted a reminder. She read the words, her ponytail fluttering in the breeze that came across the water.

"In Philae there's a place
where the priests have left no trace,
no footprints on the floor,
no divinity to adore."

The boats reached a landing stage and the passengers disembarked and went onto the island, where an Egyptian guide related the history of the temple back to the time of the pharaoh Ptolemy.

The group was then taken through lofty colonnades, through courtyards lined with decorated columns, through a massive stone pylon showing the pharaoh grasping his enemies by the hair, into a forecourt and through another pylon with twin towers, and finally to the entrance of the temple of Isis. It was flanked by goddesses carved in stone that dazzled in the sunlight. The images of the goddesses with their solar crowns were deeply incised in the stone of the towers, their forms revealed in rippling curves of shadow.

Next they were led into the dimness of the temple, and from there to the darkened sanctuary of a shrine pierced by the light that came from two tiny windows. Motes of dust danced in the light and in the torchbeams of the visitors who crowded into the place.

"And here, in the innermost holy of holies, the golden image of the goddess Isis would have stood, although sadly it is now gone, stolen in antiquity," the guide said in a hushed voice. "Imagine it," he went on. "The high priest comes in, washes and adorns the golden statue of the goddess, and makes his daily offerings to her. Afterwards he backs out of the shrine, wiping away his footprints on the floor with a palm branch."

He re-enacted the ancient ritual, bowing before an imaginary statue and then, as he backed away, sweeping an imaginary palm branch across the stone floor like a brush to remove his footsteps.

Josh remembered the wailing figure of the goddess Isis, mourning over the loss of the mummy of her husband Osiris in the Mummy Monster Game. This was her shrine. But it was empty now, except for the carved reliefs and hieroglyphics on the walls.

They moved on.

The guide stopped and pointed to a symbol that was cut deeply into the stone wall. It looked familiar. Josh was puzzled. A Christian cross in a circle? Here?

"Here in the apse of the temple of Isis, we see signs of the occupation of Philae by Christians who used it as a church in the sixth century AD," the guide said. "The Christians are gone now, but we can see traces of their worship." He pointed to a stone. "Here we see the altar, and up there the cross."

Their guided tour complete, the passengers were given free time to explore the site on their own and to take pictures if they wished.

The three children wandered outside, away from the main temple complex. Josh felt dazed, as much by the impact of the temple as by the bright sunshine. Harry led them towards a building at the edge of the island. It looked like another small temple, with its stone columns linked by carved screen walls.

"This little building is known as Pharaoh's Bed," Harry said, going inside.

"Feel like a lie down, Harry?" Amy joked.

"Not in here. But it looks like a nice quiet spot to stop and have a think."

Inside, the building was open to the sky.

"Quite a bed," Amy said admiringly, looking up at the stone columns that supported the stone architraves. She counted the columns. "A fourteen-poster!"

"We've got to think," Harry said. "We've seen most of the island now. Any clues to help us solve the riddles?"

They looked at each other.

"Nothing," Amy said.

"What have we learnt?" Josh said.

"There were Christians here once, and they left a cross," Amy said.

"That's right, and now they've gone and taken their religion with them," Harry said. "So there's nothing here to worship any more. Remember what the riddle said—*no divinity to adore.*"

"Yes, but the riddle says there's no trace and we know there *is* a trace of where they worshipped. We saw the cross and the altar."

"Maybe it's Isis who has gone," Amy said thoughtfully.

"No." Harry shook his head. "We saw carvings of her all over the walls."

"Hang on a minute," Josh said. "Amy's just reminded me of something. Think of the riddle. We're supposed to find the place where the *priests* have left no trace."

"How does that help, Josh?"

"Remember being inside the shrine? Remember what the guide said about the high priest performing his ceremony?"

"The high priest washed and dressed the golden statue of the goddess and made offerings to her," Harry said.

"Yes, but *afterwards*."

"Good one, Josh. I know where you're heading," Amy said, nodding. "After attending to the goddess, the priest backed away, wiping away all trace of his footsteps with a palm branch."

"Exactly."

Amy dipped into the pocket of her jeans and brought out the scrap of paper. "*In Philae there's a place where the priests have left no trace, no footprints on the floor, no divinity to adore.* It all fits."

"Let's go back," Harry said.

They ran back to the temple and entered the dimness of the shrine. It was empty now. They shone their torches around the walls, lighting up the reliefs, the carved figures of divinities and pharaohs making offerings. The air was thick with mystery.

"You're right, Josh. This *is* the place we had to find. The riddle said there was no goddess to adore—and there isn't. The golden statue of Isis vanished from here long ago. Well done, brother."

"You gave me the idea."

"But how does this help us find the lost pharaoh's tomb?" Harry said.

"I don't know. Maybe the game will tell us."

"Then we'll have to wait," Harry said. "We're not going back to the boat until after our second visit. We're off on a flight to Abu Simbel next."

The shrine of the temple of Isis was the right answer, Josh was sure, but the image of the priest set up an echo in his mind. Something was reverberating like a shout in an empty room. What was it? He'd have to think about it more.

6

Giants in the Desert

The excursion to Abu Simbel was only a half-hour flight from Aswan, but it took them deep into Africa, into the sun-blasted desert that was Nubia.

They took a coach to the archaeological site and walked around a mountain, and suddenly they saw them: four giants in the desert. The visitors craned their necks to gaze up at the rock-cut facade where four colossal statues of the pharaoh Rameses sat enthroned in sandstone, gazing serenely over the shimmer of Lake Nasser.

"Here we have big statues of Rameses," the guide announced. "Sixty-five feet or twenty metres high. They were built to glorify the pharaoh Rameses and establish his dominion over Nubia, and also to frighten the inhabitants who might have considered attacking southern Egypt."

If the statues were meant to strike awe into the hearts of the enemy, they certainly succeeded, Josh thought. He craned his neck to look up at one of the crowned heads of Rameses soaring high above him. Each statue seemed as tall as a five-storey building.

The second king of the four had lost his head and

shoulders, which lay collapsed in great chunks of stone at his feet.

The guide explained. "Perhaps there was an earthquake. There is uncertainty about when the catastrophe occurred, but it is my belief that it happened at the end of the last dynasty, and coincidentally marked the fall of the pharaohs. In early Christian times the pieces were buried in sand."

Josh's gaze moved up to another of the figures. As he was studying it, a falcon appeared over the top of the mountain and circled over the head of one of the pharaohs before sailing back out of view behind the mountain.

"Weird," Harry breathed. "The falcon was the ancient Egyptian symbol of kingship, and it's flying over the pharaoh's head. Here it comes again." The bird, its wing-tip feathers grabbing the air like claws, hooked into the blue sky and wheeled itself in a tight but graceful arc above the stone head of Rameses. "It's as if the spirit of the pharaoh is still watching over him."

Josh looked up at the bulging stone legs of the pharaoh. Between them stood diminutive statues of his family, charming figures standing with one foot thrust forward in the traditional Egyptian pose. Their small size—their heads did not even come up to their lord's knees—emphasised the might and godliness of the pharaoh.

"This entire mountain is artificial," the tour guide told the group of visitors. "In one of the biggest archaeological rescue missions the world has ever seen, the whole temple was cut into blocks and raised seventy metres from its old position where it was threatened by the rising waters of the Aswan Dam."

The guide, Aunt Jillian and a group of other people started to move towards the entrance to the temple, a deep black shadow cut into the rock.

The three children followed, entering the temple between two of the giant seated pharaohs. They passed through the coolness of stone and into a hall filled with more statues of the king carved as pillars, and with beautiful reliefs on the walls. These included a depiction of the pharaoh in his chariot at a great battle called Kadesh, where the pharaoh's dash and bravery saved the day for Egypt.

"Don't be too impressed," Aunt Jillian whispered. "Rameses is not a favourite of mine. He was a very vain king. Even though the battle of Kadesh is one of his claims to fame, the performance of the pharaoh and his army wasn't nearly as impressive as these commemorations suggest. It's mostly hollow boasting."

"All this was moved?" Amy said aloud in wonder, looking around the temple. "All these columns and carvings?" Her voice echoed.

"Every bit of it," Aunt Jillian said.

The group moved on.

Harry pulled at Josh's sleeve. "We've cracked it," he said. "Amy, come here."

"What?"

"We've just heard the answer. Remember what the riddle said? Give me the note."

Amy handed it to him and he shone his torchbeam on it:

Rameses multiplied himself
in search of lasting fame.
He fashioned four giant statues
his glory to proclaim.
He had a hundred sons and daughters
to further his proud aim,
but it is his hollow heart
that best repeats his name,
not once, not twice, not four times,
but again and again and again …

"The hollow heart bit," Harry said. "Don't you see? My mum said his victory at the battle of Kadesh was hollow."

"What about the name being repeated again and again?" Amy said dubiously.

"Well, he's famous for that battle. It's an event that's kept his name alive to this day."

"Maybe, Harry."

"What else could it be?" Harry argued. "Come on, I'll show you something more interesting. I'll take you through the mountain. There's a passage that goes right through it to the back."

"Not now," Josh said. "We don't want to miss anything."

"You don't think I've solved it," Harry said in a disappointed tone.

"We must be careful of jumping to conclusions," Josh said. "Let's carry on with the tour, just to be certain."

"You've seen it all before, Harry," Amy reminded him. "It's still new to us."

They rejoined the group and continued on the tour around the temple.

In a niche in the dim sanctuary at the rear of the building, the figures of four carved stone divinities sat against a wall.

"The temple was moved with such great care," the guide explained, "that twice a year, just as it used to do in ancient times, the rising sun's rays reach deep into the temple, shoot through the columns and strike the faces of these statues at the back. Truly an ancient wonder that is now also a modern wonder."

They visited the smaller neighbouring temple next, the temple built for the pharaoh's Queen Nefertari, but Harry was restless.

"These statues and carvings of the queen are beautiful," Amy said. "I think this is a much prettier temple than the Rameses one."

When they had finished the tour, Harry said, "Happy now? You've seen everything and there's no other answer. Now will you come with me through the mountain? Come along." He grabbed Amy's arm. Reluctantly, Josh followed.

Their fair-haired cousin led them out into the eye-squinting sunshine. They started to walk back in the direction of the large temple of Rameses, but before they reached it, Harry turned and took them to an entrance that led into the mountain.

They went down a passage and along a walkway, and suddenly they found themselves under a vast concrete dome that echoed with their footsteps. It looked like the inside of an observatory, and the walkway ran around the perimeter. The concrete dome supported the artificial mountain of landscaped rock that rose around and behind the temples.

"There were plans to put a restaurant in here," Harry said.

"Rameses is just a front!" Amy murmured. "He has a hollow heart."

"Let's give him a shout," Harry said. He cupped his hands and yelled up into the dome. "Hey—Rameses! *Rameses, Rameses, Rameses, Rameses, Rameses, Rameses* ..."

The echo stretched out like a line of kings fading into infinity ... again and again and again.

They looked at each other and suddenly they all knew.

It was the second clue.

"Sorry, guys," Harry said. "I tried to stop you looking."

"Don't feel too bad," Josh said. "You brought us here. Without you we'd *still* be looking."

7

On the Nile

Back on board the *Tutankhamun*, Josh, Harry and Amy gathered around the table in the boys' cabin.

Harry switched on the game.

"How do we feed in the answers to the riddles?" Josh asked. "There isn't a keyboard."

A map of the island of Philae bearing the words TEMPLE OF ISIS, PHILAE appeared on the screen. In one corner of the screen flashed a letter X.

"Try moving the directional button," Josh suggested.

Harry tried it. The X moved across the screen.

"X marks the spot," Amy said. "I suppose you have to move it and put it over the place where we found the answer."

Harry dragged the X across the map until it was directly above the shrine of the temple of Isis.

"There." He clicked the "fire" button.

The screen now changed to show the original map of Egypt.

But it wasn't blank any more. Two placenames had appeared on it: ASWAN and PHILAE.

"How does that help us?"

"It's starting to give us more details," Amy said. "You can't find hidden treasure if you've got a blank treasure map."

"The map's doing something else," Josh pointed out. "Look, it's shrunk since last time. The first time we saw it—on the plane—it showed the whole of Egypt, but now it's cut out the delta, Cairo and some of Lower Egypt."

"We're homing in on the target!" Harry said. "We're getting closer!"

Words now appeared on the screen: *Congratulations, you have solved the first riddle. You are rewarded with a game.*

"Great, we were right!" Harry said.

"Shall we tell Aunt Jillian what we're doing?" Amy wondered.

"No." Harry was firm. "It's our game. We must complete the quest ourselves! Who wants to play the free game? You play, Josh. You solved that puzzle."

Josh pushed the start button, and the pacy adventure music began. The computer seemed alive in his hands, like a beating heart, and he could feel the vibration of the music bouncing out of the tiny speaker.

"That's you," Harry said, pointing to the screen where a figure stood in a passageway. The little character, an archaeologist dressed in khaki field clothes, seemed quite unafraid as a black scorpion the size of an armoured tank scuttled through the tunnel towards him.

"Run!" Harry said.

Josh pushed the button on the left and the character took off, narrowly avoiding the scorpion's nippers. Little gold crosses with loops on top appeared like jewels above his head.

"What are those golden things hanging in the air?" Amy asked.

"They're ankhs, Egyptian crosses of life," Harry explained. "You must collect as many as you can. They'll give you extra life. Just make your character jump by hitting one of the jump buttons on the other side."

Josh tried it. The man jumped on the screen and his head went through a row of ankhs. There were twinkling sounds.

"Great, you're getting more life."

Now the obstacles began. Tomb traps.

Great blocks of stone were falling out of the ceiling. The character stopped as a block slammed down in front of him. He went around it, slowing, but the scorpion started to catch up.

What should he do?

Speed was the answer. He had to keep out of the scorpion's reach and beat the blocks of stone falling from the ceiling. Now more scorpions appeared in the passage, lying in wait for him, their poison-barbed tails raised like question marks.

A death-pit filled with spikes opened up and he jumped over it. But it slowed him, and he was nearly squashed flat by the next falling block. He had to go faster.

Josh felt himself settling into the game.

A pit appeared unexpectedly. He jumped, just in time. And then came another. The tunnel branched, and he flicked the character to one side. That lost the scorpion.

Blocks slammed down behind him. He was beating them. More ankhs hovered over him and he gathered them up. *Ping. Ping. Ping.*

"Not bad," Harry said, frowning a bit. This was the Josh of old. "Are you sure you haven't been playing games lately?"

Josh came to a hall full of columns—but the columns were really mummies who opened their bandaged arms to grab him if he ran too near them. One touched him, and his character gave an electronic squawk and seemed to jump out of its skin.

"You should be dead, but you've got extra life from the golden ankhs," said Harry.

"Thanks, ankhs," Josh said, dodging around the mummy columns. This was fun!

More blocks slammed down behind him.

Finally, he reached a doorway. There was a burst of light and words appeared: *You have won. Well played.*

The screen changed. This time it flashed up an image of a mountain temple in the desert, with four stone colossi seated in front of it. Abu Simbel.

"Our second riddle hunt," Josh said. "Let's see what that tells us."

"First we must find the hollow mountain," Harry said.

He moved the flashing x to the entrance that led to the hollow dome, and clicked.

A little red fish swam across the game display, blowing a stream of bubbles.

Red herring, red herring, red herring.

"Rameses is a red herring!" Harry laughed.

"Let's find tomorrow's clues," Josh suggested.

Harry pressed the play buttons and new words appeared on the screen. *You have earned a bonus riddle for solving two clues. This is not a clue to find at your next site, but a key to the whole mystery:*

Sail like a mummy on its pilgrimage cruise,
but was it a visit—or merely a ruse?

"Write it down," Harry said.

Josh scribbled the riddle on a piece of paper.

The game moved on to give them the riddle for their visit to Kom Ombo:

To find this new location
may seem an operation.
A wall shows signs of healing:
you will know it by your feeling.

Josh wrote this on the scrap of paper too.

They did not have much time to think about these new clues, however. A bell rang out through the boat and all passengers were called to the lounge for a fire safety drill.

That evening, Josh sat next to Amy and Harry at Aunt Jillian's lecture, scribbling notes on a pad.

Aunt Jillian pushed a button on her slide projector and flashed up a picture of a ruined temple in the desert.

"This was the next step in my detective chase for the missing tomb of pharaoh Heri-hor," she said. "This is his funerary cenotaph or temple out in the desert beyond Abydos. Not much of it is left now, just part of the shrine, a few broken columns and the Nilometer that once adjoined it."

"Cool," Josh muttered.

"Abydos is the oldest sacred city in Egypt, and the Nile's most important archaeological site," Aunt Jillian went on. "It was believed to be the site of the Staircase of the God Osiris, Lord of the Underworld. He was the mummy god who held out the promise of resurrection to every Egyptian who had lived a good life. The original god of Abydos was a mysterious figure called the Opener of Ways, symbolised by a jackal—jackals can still be seen slinking around the cemeteries on the desert fringe. His name was Wepwawet. Later he was joined in the Egyptian pantheon by another god known as Foremost of the Westerners, who in turn was combined in the godhead of Osiris."

Amy looked at Josh as he fidgeted in his chair. Aunt Jillian continued.

"Now, it is certain that the body of my missing pharaoh Heri-hor would have rested here in this temple cenotaph for a time before being taken back to the Valley of the Kings for burial."

A question reared in Josh's mind. He shot up his hand.

"Yes, Josh?" Aunt Jillian said, surprised.

Amy gave him a nudge. "Shouldn't you wait till the end?" she whispered.

Some of the passengers turned to look at him.

"Er—sorry, I'll ask it afterwards," he stumbled.

"No, it's all right, Josh."

"Weren't pharaohs ever buried there? At Abydos, I mean."

"Yes, the first kings were, including the second dynasty king Djer whose tomb traditionally came to be identified with the tomb of Osiris. Tombs have been found here. But of course, in later times, pharaohs had their capitals in faraway places such as Memphis or Thebes, and it was normal for them to be buried where they had lived. It is possible that they were buried at Abydos, however, and there is much dispute over which of these temples are cenotaphs and which are mortuary temples."

"What's the difference?" Josh said.

"A cenotaph is merely commemorative. A temple suggests worship and an ongoing cult for the dead king. Mortuary temples were often in the vicinity of tombs, and a king's mummy may at least have rested in one for a period during its sacred pilgrimage visit."

"But ..." Josh hesitated.

"Yes, Josh?"

"How do you know your pharaoh isn't buried at Abydos—if Egyptians wanted to be buried as near as possible to the Staircase of the God?"

"Good question. But there are two arguments against it. First of all, the tomb at Luxor *shows* the king Herihor's body being taken to Abydos on a pilgrimage and then being taken back to the Valley of the Kings opposite Luxor. And secondly, we know he had a tomb built in the Valley ... I found it."

"But it was empty," Josh said.

"Yes, it was empty. And I found no trace of his tomb in the Necropolis—the royal cemetery at Abydos—either. I've mapped, trenched and searched the area high and low."

It was gala dinner night and the passengers of the *Tutankhamun* had dressed up for the occasion.

Aunt Jillian and Harry came in full expeditionary gear, 1930s style. They both wore khaki field clothes and old-fashioned pith helmets. Amy wore a sheer white nightgown. Aunt Jillian had helped her dress and had tied her hair in a sidelock, in the fashion worn by the princesses of ancient Egypt. Her face had been made up in the ancient Egyptian style, too, with shadowed eyelids fanning out at the corners like fishtails. She looked a little creepy, Josh thought, and she acted very cool and aloof, like a real princess.

Josh wore a white galabea which he'd bought from the shop on board. He felt as if he was wearing a dress.

The waiters all wore galabeas, too, and dinner was a smorgasbord of spicy Egyptian dishes.

Next morning, Josh was woken up by a knocking at the cabin door. He opened it, rubbing his eyes.

It was Amy, up and dressed already.

"We're moving, Josh. Come up on deck." She ran off.

Harry was still asleep, so Josh threw on some jeans and a T-shirt and joined Amy on the deck.

The *Tutankhamun* had already left the other tourist boats that crowded the quay at Aswan. Josh looked about at the broad, shining expanse of the Nile. The stark, caramel-coloured hills of the Tombs of the Nomarchs caught the first glow in the sky. Tombs were never very far away in Egypt, Aunt Jillian had said: they opened up everywhere, like doorways to eternity. Yet it was hard to think of dying and eternity on such a hopeful morning.

A fresh wind blew from the north and a felucca loaded with stone leaned into it, its sail cutting a wedge in the blue-green of the river. The boatman, dressed in a grey galabea, held a long white tiller. Countless palm trees raised their heads above a thick belt of greenery on the river's edge. They passed thickets of reeds, but these were not papyrus, Amy informed Josh. According to her guide book, papyrus had all but vanished from the Nile in Egypt and could only be found further south in the Sudan and the marshes of the Sudd.

A falcon planed over the waters, greeting the dawn.

They berthed at the quay at Kom Ombo after breakfast. As they walked up to the temple they passed a plot of ground where a farmer worked the land in the age-old manner, guiding a wooden plough behind two oxen.

Josh, Amy and Harry walked together behind the group of passengers.

"What was that clue again?" Amy asked.

Josh read it out.

"To find this new location
may seem an operation.
A wall shows signs of healing:
you will know it by your feeling."

They learned from their guide that the temple of Kom Ombo, built in the Graeco-Roman period, was rare in that it was actually two temples, split along an imaginary line. One half was dedicated to Horus, the falcon-headed god, and the other half to Sobek, the crocodile god. Until as recently as a hundred years earlier, the region of Kom Ombo had been infested with crocodiles, the guide explained.

Josh allowed himself to be carried along by the chattering flow of the commentary. They meandered on a river of history among forecourts, columned halls, and vestibules. They paused at columns and walls with deeply cut carvings of Horus and the crocodile-headed god Sobek, gathering to listen as the guide stopped to explain the hieroglyphics. He pointed out a carving of Ptolemy, one of several pharaohs called by that name, who had built this temple.

Josh felt dreamy and removed from himself. He enjoyed hearing about this place. It was as if the knowledge was awakening something in his mind that had long lain untouched.

Learning things *could* be interesting. The mystery of Egypt was reaching out to him.

The guide led them into a small shrine and showed them mummified crocodiles lying in a glass case. "These crocodiles come from a nearby crocodile cemetery," he told them.

Josh stared at the three small, unbandaged crocodiles. They looked like stuffed crocodiles in a natural history museum. Aunt Jillian pointed at them and murmured,

"These mummified animals can be more valuable than people think. They were often stuffed with scraps of papyrus that had writings on them. Through these scraps we have sometimes obtained the endings to texts that have been missing for thousands of years. It was in one of these that I first found the document from the architect Setekhy that led to the discovery of his tomb. It recorded permission from the pharaoh for him to build his own tomb."

Josh put his face to the glass and wondered what secrets lay hidden inside these small crocodiles. Egypt seemed to be dense with secrets.

In an outer corridor on the northern side of the temple, the guide stopped to point out some carvings on a wall.

"Can anybody tell me what we are looking at here?" he asked. Incised into the stone was the image of a table and, on top of it, a box displaying a set of strange looking instruments which looked to Josh like carpenter's tools.

One man said, "They look like surgical instruments."

"Very good," the guide nodded. "See here: scalpels, cutting instruments, lancets and tongs ..."

Amy made a face. "Some of those things look painful," she said.

"The ancient Egyptians were very advanced in medicine," the guide told them. "For example, a papyrus has been found that prescribes a treatment for sword wounds. It recommends that the fungus from the underside of a certain lily be applied to heal the wound. Penicillin, many thousands of years ago."

When the tour was over, the three children gathered to discuss their ideas.

Josh consulted the note. He read out the first part: "*To find this new location may seem an operation.* I suppose that's telling us it's pretty hard to find."

"It is," Harry said. "It's got me."

"What's the last part again?" Amy said.

"*A wall shows signs of healing: you will know it by your feeling.*"

"I suppose it means there's a wall that's been restored. But I'll bet most of this temple has been restored at some time or another."

"*You will know it by your feeling,*" Amy repeated thoughtfully. "What feelings did we have?"

"I enjoyed the feeling of walking through here," Josh said.

"No, I think it has to be a specific feeling." She thought about it. "What do you feel?"

"Confused," Harry said.

"Stuck," Josh said.

The guide called the passengers to return to the boat.

"Come on, think," Josh said, more to himself than the others.

"No, feel," Amy said. "The only thing I felt was a shiver when I saw the carving of those instruments." Then she stopped and her clear grey eyes widened. "The instruments! Surgical instruments! The riddle's a play on words. That's what the 'operation' means."

"And the wall shows signs of healing!" Josh quoted the rest. "It refers to instruments used in healing! Of course! Brilliant, Amy."

"That was amazing, Amy," Harry said, smiling, but

almost grumbling. "Give us a chance."

"I'm glad we've solved it," Josh said. "Now we can relax and take a wander around the temple."

It was a lovely lazy morning on the cruise boat. Its golden bow and stern gleamed in the sunlight, and the river was green and silver.

After a swim in the pool, Josh sat with Harry, Amy and Aunt Jillian, high up on the top deck under a shady canopy, watching the river slide by.

He dug into his shirt pocket and pulled out a scrap of paper. It was the clue for their next destination, the temple of Edfu.

The Kom Ombo riddle had produced a red fish on the screen. Yet another red herring, blowing empty bubbles.

Again, the next clue was a riddle. Josh had written it down with an eager hand. It's only a game, he told himself. But the coincidences were beginning to excite him.

He read the riddle on the scrap of paper.

Where the temple serpent
spirals down to drink,
remember this clue:
you're on the brink.
Cold as stone,
covered in scale,
press for the secret:
you must not fail.

"Egypt is a very fortunate land," Aunt Jillian told

them, enjoying the cooling breeze. "As a famous Greek historian, Herodotus, said, 'Egypt is the gift of the Nile'. In ancient times, the country's fortunes rose or fell depending on the level of the river's annual flood. A low Nile meant disaster and famine. A good Nile, prosperity and joy."

Josh was surprised to see how uninhabited Egypt seemed in places. There were great empty stretches of river bank between villages, although most of this land was under cultivation. A surprising number of islands were dotted along the Nile, too. He wondered if there were buried temples or tombs on them.

They saw a boatman out on the water. He had a long pole in his hands and he was smacking it down hard on the surface of the water to frighten fish into his waiting net.

"That is a scene straight out of an ancient tomb painting," Aunt Jillian said.

Two feluccas slipped by, tied together side by side, their sails like white triangles as they bent over in the wind. Every now and then the *Tutankhamun* passed other cruise boats on the Nile, boats with names like *Isis Island* and *Nile Pearl*. The cruise boat captains always greeted other boats with three loud toots, and never seemed to tire of doing it.

Aunt Jillian pointed out how suddenly the green belt of cultivation at the edge of the Nile gave way to the desert beyond.

"The Nile isn't just a river running through Egypt," she said. "It *is* Egypt. The knife-edge division between the greenery and the western and eastern deserts always startles me, even after all these years—it's like the sharp sunlight and shadow of Egypt. Maybe it was features like these that made the Egyptians so aware of the boundary between life and death."

"I can't understand why the Egyptian pharaohs took all their treasures to the grave with them if they were going to another life," Amy said.

"Maybe they wanted a little travel insurance," Aunt Jillian joked. "No, they believed they could enjoy all these things again in the next life."

Josh still looked forward to going into his first tomb, but he would have to wait till they reached Luxor. In the meantime there were more stops on the river.

More clues to gather.

After lunch they would visit the temple of Horus at Edfu. Josh thought about the clue: *Where the temple serpent spirals down to drink ...*

"Excuse me," he said, getting up. "I'm going to change."

He went below decks to the small book-lined library. No one else was there.

He chose two books, one about the discovery of the tomb of the boy king Tutankhamun by the Egyptologist Howard Carter, the other about Egyptian mythology, and he took them over to the reading table.

He opened the book on Tutankhamun first. Inside were photographs of breathtaking treasures: the golden mummy mask he had seen in the Cairo museum, the golden coffin case, furniture, pieces of gleaming jewellery. As he turned the pages, he felt again the stirring of a new interest: a fascination with mystery and knowledge and unknown possibilities. He had never thought of it until this trip, but learning *could* be an adventure.

Maybe this is a new direction for me, he thought. The idea intrigued him. He felt as Howard Carter must have felt when he found that first stone step hidden in the sand, one tantalising step that led to unknown riches below. He read with growing excitement about the discovery of the boy king's tomb.

Then he turned to the book on ancient Egyptian mythology and read about mythological creatures, in particular serpents and monsters.

He learned about the serpent named Apophis, also known as the Great Worm, a creature of heart-stopping proportions. The Egyptians believed that by day the sun sailed across the sky in a boat, and at night it travelled through the underworld. Apophis attacked the sun boat every morning and evening. An eclipse meant that the serpent had triumphed, swallowing the sun or the moon. Apophis, Josh read, was a demon creature linked with Seth, the Egyptian god of chaos and destruction.

He came across an illustration of the great serpent. It was a wall relief from a length of corridor in a pharaoh's tomb and it showed the creature throwing its rippling coils over a sun boat. On the same page was a depiction of Seth, showing his animal head with its upraised, square-tipped ears and drooping snout.

Into Josh's mind drifted an image of the face of a man. A man with a long, hooked nose ... *The man in the little games shop in Cairo.*

He remembered the snarling image of Seth in the

window of the games shop.

That's right, they *had* looked the same. A creepy coincidence?

He jotted down a few notes.

8

The Serpent in the Temple

They travelled by horse-drawn carriage through the small, crowded town of Edfu to the temple of Horus.

"Don't beat the horses or I won't pay you," Aunt Jillian warned the driver, who put away his whip with a grin and flicked the reins. The carriage, called a gharry, was shiny black on the outside and decorated inside with coloured pictures of American movie stars cut from a magazine. Josh guessed that it was meant to make foreigners feel at home.

Hawkers and children besieged the visitors when they climbed out of their carriage. A small boy in a striped galabea ran up to Harry. "One pound, one pound!" he said, with his hand stuck out.

"Pens, pens," a young girl said to Amy.

"Why pens?" Amy asked.

"These children have an insatiable desire for ballpoint pens," said Aunt Jillian.

Amy dragged a pen from her pocket and gave it to the girl. She received it like a prize, beaming at Amy.

"One, pound, one pound," the little boy demanded of Harry.

"I haven't got a pound. How about a toffee instead?" Harry said, handing one over. The boy seemed quite satisfied.

They went through a market crowded with hawkers selling an array of curios: miniature jackals, falcons, crocodiles and mummy cases; galabeas, printed fabrics and jewellery.

The temple of Edfu, the best preserved temple in Egypt, was partly surrounded by mud brick walls. They passed around the side of the temple and along a walkway inside the brick wall to the front of the building. The facade was a magnificent sight. It looked like a giant's fortress, guarded by a stupendous stone pylon with two towers. Flanking the entrance were large granite statues of falcons representing the god Horus. The birds were streamlined and angry-eyed.

Entering the pylon between the towers, they came to a vast court bordered by columns and then went through a doorway, guarded by another stone falcon, into a series of dim hypostyle halls, each with a stone roof supported by pillars.

Josh looked up at the bulging, rounded columns. Some were topped with palm-motif capitals, others with open papyrus heads, or with closed buds.

Light from slanting apertures high in the roof lit hieroglyphs and carvings of a pharaoh making offerings to gods and goddesses.

The chambers became progressively darker until the visitors found themselves in the shrine. The guide showed them trapdoors that led to crypts beneath the temple.

"This crypt led to the Nilometer which once linked up to the Nile—a secret swift passage into the temple of Horus," he informed the group. "But today it is no longer linked with the Nile."

"Wow!" Harry said. "A secret passage that led all the way to the Nile!"

"What's a Nilometer?" Josh asked the guide.

"It is a deep shaft with a staircase going down the inside. It was used to measure the height of the river's annual flood."

"The Nile, here in the temple?" Josh said thoughtfully.

"Let's go and look at it," Amy said after the tour. She had her guide book with her. "I think I can find it."

Amy led them to the second columned hall, into an area called the ambulatory, and along a wall decorated with reliefs. Then, taking out their torches, they descended a staircase that spiralled down into what seemed like a well.

"Slowly!" Josh called to Harry, who was racing ahead. His voice echoed down the Nilometer and up again. The guide had said that the shaft was no longer linked with the Nile, but there was still black, evil looking water at the bottom of the staircase. Perhaps it had flooded after a storm, Josh thought, flashing his torchlight around in search of a clue.

"Maybe there's a carving of the serpent Apophis here."

"Apophis?" Amy said. "Who's Apophis?"

"Something I read about in the library."

"You were in the library?"

"Don't sound so surprised."

"I'm impressed. Anyway, who's Apophis?"

"The great serpent of the Egyptian underworld," Harry put in. "Mum told me all about it."

Lighting the walls with their torches, they saw a scale to measure the height of the river, and some ancient hieroglyphs.

"Nothing here," Amy said.

"Maybe we missed it in the temple," Harry said.

They ran up the spiral steps of the Nilometer and went back to the temple. Josh re-checked the riddle.

Where the temple serpent
spirals down to drink,
remember this clue:
you're on the brink.
Cold as stone,
covered in scale,
press for the secret:
you must not fail.

They searched for a carving of a serpent going down to drink. They checked on stone columns, in small chapels, in hypostyle halls and courtyards. They even checked outside the temple, going along a narrow space between the temple and an outer wall. The temple wall was decorated with inscriptions and reliefs showing Horus in a boat on the Nile. Armed with a spear, he was battling his ancient enemy Seth, who had assumed the form of a hippopotamus.

By now it was growing late, and the guide was calling the group together to return to the boat.

"It's no good, we have to go," Amy said disappointedly.

They looked at each other, hoping somebody would have an idea.

Does it matter? Josh thought. It's only a game. Or is it? Somehow, what was happening in the game and what was happening in real life seemed to be converging like railway lines in the distance. Maybe it was that kind of illusion.

They would have to find that elusive horizon where the two lines met.

Back on the boat, they switched on the game.

A map of the temple of Edfu appeared, and a letter X blinking in the corner of the screen urged them to select a site.

"What happens if we get it wrong and skip one of the clues?" Amy said.

"We break the chain, I'd say," Josh said. "Maybe the game will stop giving us any more clues."

"We've got to get it right," Harry said anxiously.

Amy sighed. "We probably saw the answer to the riddle, and didn't even realise it."

"We can't guess," Josh said. "We'll just have to keep thinking."

9

Mummies, Mummies

"This is a worry," Harry said as they stood on the deck watching the *Tutankhamun* moor at the quay. They were about to go ashore at Esna, their next site on the Nile, but they still had not solved the last riddle. "We're slipping behind," he continued. "We haven't worked out the last clue, and now we haven't been told what to look for here."

From the quay, they had to walk through a narrow lane between mud brick buildings. The lane was filled with clamouring street hawkers selling curios and souvenirs.

A tall, bony man with a hooked nose thrust a statue in front of Josh's face. "Five pound, five pound."

Josh gave a start as he recognised the statue's familiar features—the hooked nose and square-tipped ears of the animal-headed god Seth. And the hawker himself looked exactly like the man from the games shop in Cairo.

It couldn't be. Just a spooky resemblance, Josh decided. "No thanks."

A shyly grinning old man with a gap in his teeth followed Amy all the way to the temple, saying, "Mummies,

mummies" in a singsong way. He held a miniature carved mummy case made of stone, with a loose lid.

"Mummies, mummies, pretty girl."

"No thank you," Amy said politely.

The temple of Esna sat in a hole, way below the level of the mud brick town which had built up around it in many layers over thousands of years. It was a pretty temple, with its roof intact, and it was filled with birds that fluttered among the sculpted columns.

On the way out, the guide signalled the group of passengers to gather around, and he pointed sorrowfully at the foundations of the temple.

"The Aswan Dam has changed the water table," he said, shaking his head, "and now the salt comes up to eat away the monuments. Just three months ago I was at this site. Since then a small carving has already vanished. It was right here, but has flaked off with the rising salt crystals."

He showed a blank spot in a wall relief.

Amy seemed distracted. She looked up at the entrance, above the steps that came down into the hole. The old man stood at the top of the steps, waving his mummy case.

"Mummies, mummies!" he called.

"How much?" Amy said, on the way out of the temple.

"You very pretty girl." The old man smiled, showing the gap in his teeth. "And you very handsome, man, sir," he said to Harry,

"Thank you, but the price," Amy said.

"This very fine mummy."

"Yes, but the price ..."

"How much you pay for this fine mummy case? Look." He made the lid and the small coffin base rattle like false teeth between his fingers.

"Say a price," Amy said to the man.

"He wants you to make an offer," Harry said.

"Two pounds," Amy said, reaching into her jeans pocket for her money.

"Very fine mummy."

"Three ..."

"Special mummy."

"Four."

He nodded, pressed the mummy into her hand. "You take it for five," he said with an air of concession.

"Five?" Amy said. "Where did five come from?" The old man grinned in a winning way and Amy had to smile too. She shrugged.

"I'd like it as a keepsake. And five Egyptian pounds isn't very much."

She parted with the money and went off with her miniature stone mummy case.

The three were glum by the time they boarded the boat.

Now they had missed two riddle locations in the game, Josh thought. They were falling hopelessly behind.

Forget Esna, he told himself. Go back and try to solve the Edfu riddle. Once again he ran the words of the riddle through his mind.

Where the temple serpent
spirals down to drink,

remember this clue:
you're on the brink.

Words, that's all they were. Or were they?

Maybe he should think about the problem in a different way. The riddle described a picture, too.

Josh found a pencil and some paper in his cabin.

"What are you doing?" Harry said.

"Drawing?"

"Drawing what?"

"Drawing on another side of my brain."

Harry and Amy leaned over him as he sketched a temple in profile.

Where the temple serpent spirals down.

Down.

Must be a hole.

He sketched a shaft going down below the temple.

Where the serpent spirals down to drink.

Spirals down.

Don't think it. Draw it.

He drew a spiralling snake going down the shaft.

Then he put down the pencil and laughed.

"Look!" he said. He hadn't drawn a serpent going down into a hole. He had drawn something different, which they all remembered.

The Nilometer at Edfu.

"The answer's the Nilometer," he said jubilantly. "It's the staircase that spirals down like a snake. And it isn't going down to drink, it's going down to meet the Nile! It isn't a serpent at all. It's a thingo."

"A metaphor," Amy said.

"Right."

"Well done, Josh!" Amy said, deeply impressed.

"That's brilliant thinking, Josh!" Harry thumped his cousin on the back.

"I don't know about brilliant thinking, but it's not bad drawing," Josh smiled.

"I wonder if it's a red herring?" Harry said.

"I hope it isn't, after all that work."

"Try it out," Amy said.

Josh picked up the game gear and turned it on. He pressed the directional button and slid the X across the map to the detail of the Nilometer that jutted out from the temple walls.

He clicked over the circular staircase, shown in plan section.

Correct. A valuable clue. You are on the brink.

Harry and Amy cheered, and a grin spread across Josh's face.

The trail of clues was unbroken!

"Look what the game's saying!"

He read out the words that had appeared on the LCD display: "*Congratulations. You are closer than ever to finding the forgotten pharaoh's tomb.*"

"I knew it! We're getting close!" Harry said. "We mustn't give up now. What do you think, Josh?"

"The map's moved in even tighter. Look. Lower and Middle Egypt have almost disappeared. I think we're very close. Maybe it's in Luxor in the Valley of the Kings, where they found the tomb of Tutankhamun."

Once again the map reduced in area, losing all of Middle Egypt. It now showed the town of Edfu.

Your reward is a game, the display told them.

The screen changed to another platform game and adventure music started up.

"Who wants to play?" Josh said. "I need to give my head a rest."

"Do you want to play, Amy?"

She sat on the edge of a bed.

"No thanks. I want to look at my mummy case." She inspected the tiny stone coffin, taking off the lid. "It'll make a great pencil case," she said.

Harry took the game gear, and Josh watched as he ran the small archaeologist character through a series of pyramids. It was a tricky run, made trickier by an ever-present wall of sharp steel spikes. Some flights of stairs went up and some went down. Up and down, up and down he went. Sometimes, when he thought the stairs were going up, he found they were actually going down because the pyramid had suddenly turned upside-down, playing tricks with gravity. As long as he kept going very fast, he could run upside down without falling and landing on the steel spikes.

"Sometimes up is down and sometimes down is up. The stairs go both ways," Harry said.

"Stairs usually do, Harry," Josh said.

When the game sequence was finished, Harry pushed the play button. They still needed to catch up with Esna.

Now a different map appeared. This time it was a town. Looking more closely, they saw what appeared to be the plan of a temple inside the town.

"What have we got to look for this time?"

A riddle appeared on the display:

The answer soars above some heads,
though under merchants' feet.
Once it reached up to the heavens,
now it's reduced to a lowly street.

"*The answer soars above some heads*," Amy murmured, "*though under merchants' feet.* That reminds me of when I was standing in the temple. When I looked up, I could see the merchant's feet—the one who sold me this mummy case."

Josh caught her meaning at once. He repeated the last words of the riddle out loud: "*Once it reached up to the heavens, now it's reduced to a lowly street.*"

"It's the temple of Esna!" Harry said. "The temple has sunk to below the level of the town! Good one, Amy!"

"That cute old man with the mummy case made me think of it," Amy said. "I'm glad I bought it from him now, and I'm glad I gave him the price he wanted. I was really glad anyway," she added.

But they still hadn't pinpointed a target.

"How do we choose a whole temple when we've only got an X?" Harry said. "It isn't one part of the temple this time."

"Just try clicking it all over the temple. It'll get the message."

It did.

"We've got it!" Harry said.

Now they were keen to discover the next clue: it would be about Luxor, site of the Valley of the Kings and the most famous tombs in Egypt. Soon it appeared on the screen:

There are crooked steps that you must follow
or your quest for me will turn out hollow.
To the underworld up in the air
take the journey, for my tomb is there.

No individual site map appeared, just several dots on the map on either side of the river in the region where the town of Luxor lay.

"Crooked steps, underworld up in the air ..." Josh said, puzzled. "What does it mean?"

"Sounds like stairs to the Egyptian heaven," Amy said, taking a guess.

"Or the Staircase of the God," Josh said. "I remember Aunt Jillian mentioning it in her talk."

Harry was still puzzled. "Well, we're not going to find a real staircase to heaven, are we? Maybe it's a picture of one, something in the tombs we'll be visiting tomorrow."

They spent the night moored at Esna and Aunt Jillian gave another lecture, this time about Howard Carter's discovery of the tomb of king Tutankhamun. Josh, who had read about it in the library, enjoyed it all over again.

In the morning, they passed through a barrage on the Nile and then cruised to Luxor.

Mountains of golden, sunburnt rock rose into view on the western side of the river as they neared the busy town. The quay was jammed with gleaming Nile cruisers. The *Tutankhamun* berthed alongside six others in a row, and the passengers had to walk through the reception areas of each boat to reach the shore.

Luxor smelled of horse manure. Horse-drawn gharries were everywhere. The group spent the afternoon exploring the temple of Luxor, which looked like a picture postcard temple, Josh thought, especially when the sun went down behind the pylons and the seated statues of Rameses, and the light faded over a long line of ram-headed sphinxes.

They were up at five o'clock the next morning, and as the sun rose they set off across the Nile by ferry to visit the Valley of the Kings and the Valley of the Queens. The mist-enshrouded river had a dreamlike quality, creating the perfect mood for visiting the Land of the Dead.

On the other side of the river they boarded a coach and travelled through canefields and past two vast seated statues—the statues of Memnon—that sat alone in a field.

"Once they stood in front of a temple," Aunt Jillian told them, "the funerary temple of Amenhotep the Third. It vanished long ago. After an earthquake in 27 BC, these stone statues started to emit a peculiar sound like singing. It happened every morning, when the sun's rays first warmed the stone. But they were repaired some time later and have been silent ever since."

The first tomb they approached, that of a young prince,

lay in the Valley of the Queens. Because the tombs were dusty, tourists were given paper masks to wear over their noses and mouths.

They slipped on their masks and went down a flight of steps into a long narrow tomb. A painted underworld enveloped them in a blaze of colour. Wonderful images of the young prince, shaven headed except for a plaited sidelock of youth like a tail at the side of his head, enlivened the walls. The colours of the murals looked as fresh as they must have been when the artist had just finished painting them.

Josh now understood Aunt Jillian's comment at the beginning of the cruise. This tomb wasn't scary at all. It was as brightly decorated as a nursery. There were touches of humour too: one scene showed a queen tickling the pharaoh under the chin with a long finger.

"It all looks so alive!" Amy said in delight.

Next they visited the tomb of a workman named Sennedjem, who had helped to build the royal tombs. The low ceiling was painted to look like a vineyard with hanging clusters of grapes. Josh felt he could reach up and pick a bunch.

The highlight of this tour was a visit to the Valley of the Kings, an impressive, silent spot encircled by hills and overlooked by a peak shaped like a pyramid.

"That peak was a goddess," the tour guide told them. "She was Meretseger, a protector of the dead, who could also assume the form of a serpent. She was known as the Lover of Silence."

Aunt Jillian added her own comment to the children

in a whisper: "The silence of this spot also gave the dead some protection against robbers. You can hear a pin drop here, and the sound of metal hitting rock carries for kilometres."

At last they went inside a real pharaoh's tomb, deeply cut in the rock. It was the tomb of Amenhotep the Second. After walking down steep steps and a sloping corridor, they came suddenly upon a pit spanned by a bridge. They paused on the bridge and peered nervously into the shadowy void. The bridge had been built in recent times to allow access to the tomb.

"Was this a trap built to catch robbers?" Josh asked Aunt Jillian.

"Possibly," she said. "But it also acted as a sump to collect water if a flash flood threatened the tomb."

They reached a chamber in which there were six pillars painted with scenes of the pharaoh meeting the gods, and walls filled with mystical scenes of the pharaoh in the underworld. Texts were painted on a yellow background like papyrus.

Was the answer to the riddle here?

They scoured the walls for something that might represent a stairway to heaven or the Staircase of the God.

At the back of this chamber was the crypt, where the king's sandstone sarcophagus still stood.

"This was the tomb of not one, but many pharaohs," Aunt Jillian said. "In spite of all the protection, the ancient keepers of the Necropolis discovered that many of the tombs had been broken into by tomb-robbers and the mummies torn apart by greedy thieves searching for gold and jewellery." She pointed to two side-chambers. "In order to save the remaining mummies, the keepers brought a collection of them here to this tomb, which had remained hidden from robbers. Imagine a council of dead kings gathered together in this underground silence, not only Amenhotep the Second, but Amenhotep the Third, Thutmosis the Fourth, Siptah and Seti the Second."

"They came for a sleepover," Harry laughed.

"I wonder how poor Amenhotep felt," Amy said. "He thought he had a private room."

After the tomb of Amenhotep, they visited the tombs of four different kings named Rameses and the tomb of Mereneptah, said by some to be the pharaoh mentioned in the Book of Exodus. In one of the tombs—the tomb of Rameses the Third—they found people from the Egyptian Antiquities Organisation working on paintings to preserve them. A friendly official, kneeling at the foot of a wall with an artist's paintbrush in his hand, saw Amy staring with interest at what they were doing. He called her over, gave her his paintbrush, and invited her to dip it into a jar of liquid.

"Me?"

He nodded. "You do it."

The man pointed to the foot of a painted goddess. It was faded and flaky looking. Amy knelt. She dipped the fine brush in the liquid and leaned forward.

Scarcely daring to breathe, she carefully dabbed the tip of the brush on the toe of the goddess. Fresh colour sprang up. Amy went on to another toe and then to the rest of the foot.

Harry was impressed. "Wow! Amy's painting a pharaoh's tomb!"

"There is no pigment on the brush," the official explained. "Only silicone to seal the painting."

Amy finished the foot of the goddess.

"Good work. You get a job here—no problem," he joked.

"Thank you," Amy said gratefully to the man, giving him back his brush. Her eyes shone with delight.

"You are welcome."

"Well done, Amy," Aunt Jillian murmured, patting her on the shoulder. "You've done your bit to preserve ancient Egypt."

Amy looked thrilled, and walked through the rest of the tomb with a look of awe in her eyes. Josh felt a twinge of envy, but he was pleased for his sister.

The tomb of Tutankhamun was closed for repairs, but Aunt Jillian consoled them by explaining that they weren't missing much after all. Tutankhamun's tomb was quite small and cramped compared with the tombs they had seen, and was famous only because of the funerary goods found inside it, most of which had been taken away to the Cairo museum.

A common theme in the tombs was an image of boats, Josh noted: painted ones, carved ones, sketched ones, some floating on the underworld Nile, some in the windless underworld hauled by goddesses with ropes, some travelling like the sun through the heavens, some carrying the sarcophagus of a dead king on its pilgrimage cruise to the holy city of Abydos.

They saw nothing, however, that looked like an underworld up in the air, a stairway to heaven, or the Staircase of the God.

When the passengers were returning to the coach, Aunt Jillian took the three children aside. She gave them a choice.

"You can go with the rest of the group and visit some more temples, or you can come with me to see the tomb I discovered."

"We'll come with you," Josh said quickly, speaking for them all.

A colleague of Aunt Jillian's, a man named Amira, was waiting to take them in a four-wheel-drive vehicle to the site.

10

Aunt Jillian's Tomb

The tomb was set in a cliff, thirty metres from the ground. Zig-zagging steps, some carved, some set in place, made a giddy climb to the mouth.

"This is scary," Amy said, looking over the side.

"You should have been here when we discovered it. There were no steps then," Aunt Jillian told her. "I had to abseil down on a rope from the top of the cliff."

Amy gulped. "Abseil? Where did you learn to do things like that?"

"It's one of the necessities of my profession. There are no lifts and walkways on archaeological sites. You learn to get anywhere with a rope and a good pair of shoes. Anyway, that was easy. What's more scary is going down a tomb pit when you can't even see the bottom."

There was an iron gate at the entrance to the tomb. Amira produced a key and opened it, and they went inside. This tomb was unlit, so they turned on their torches.

This is more like it, Josh thought. Without lighting, tombs were much more mysterious places. Scenes from Aunt Jillian's slide show on the boat sprang into life in their torchbeams, as if she had pushed a button on a projector. "As you can see—empty," Aunt Jillian said, her voice echoing.

"Where is the scene of the king being taken to Abydos?" Josh asked.

"There. See the king's funerary boat?"

The painting showed an ornate funerary barge with a swept-up prow and stern, and the sarcophagus of the king lying on the deck under a canopy.

"Tell us about it again," Josh said. Something was bothering him.

Aunt Jillian explained, shining her torch on the wall. "Abydos was the holy capital of Egypt. Tradition held that the body of the man-god Osiris was buried there. It was believed therefore that the ladder to heaven—the Staircase of the God—lay in Abydos. Everybody wanted to go there on a pilgrimage. Dead kings were even taken to Abydos after their mummification. It was the desire of all Egyptians to be linked as closely as they could with the Staircase of the God. Pharaohs had commemorative chapels or temples built at Abydos."

Josh nodded. He was thinking hard.

"And over here," Aunt Jillian said, pointing to a flight of steps painted on the wall. "Who can tell me what this is?"

"It's the Staircase of the God," Josh said.

"Correct," Aunt Jillian said.

Fragments of a puzzle were tumbling in his mind. It was as if he had tossed a jigsaw into the air and was watching the pieces fall in slow motion. But they were still high up—and even if they did come down, would they ever fit together?

When they left the tomb and returned to the bottom of the cliff, Josh stopped at the foot of the zig-zag steps and looked up.

There are crooked steps that you must follow
or your quest for me will turn out hollow.
To the underworld up in the air
take the journey, for my tomb is there.

But the tomb was empty and the mummy had never been there, according to Aunt Jillian.

"I know what you're thinking," Amy said.

"So do I," Harry said glumly.

They looked at each other, mystified.

It didn't make sense.

Josh was silent on the way to the ferry and on the trip back across the Nile. They had time for a quick visit to the temple of Karnak at dusk.

It was the biggest religious complex in Egypt, Aunt Jillian told them, and one of the biggest on earth. The giant stone columns in the hypostyle halls soared to such a height that Josh gave himself a crick in the neck trying to see the top. Harry made a joke of it by gazing upwards while lying on the ground, flat on his back.

"Harry, stop fooling around," Amy laughed.

Josh enjoyed walking through the hectares of crumbling temple. They stopped for a rest beside a lake, a sheet of still water that once had carried sacred barges.

"What's on your mind Josh?" Amy asked.

"I wish I could tell you," he said, closing his eyes and trying to think. "Everything's up in the air, like pieces of a scattered jigsaw. And I can only glimpse what's on the pieces. A fact here, another fact there, and bits of things we've seen—boats, empty tombs, temples, staircases … Somehow, it all has to come together, but how?"

When they returned to the cruise boat, Harry switched on the game. The map of the Luxor region appeared on the screen.

They looked at the dots on the map.

"Where's Mum's tomb?" Harry said.

"Over here, I'd say." Josh pointed. "This would be the Valley of the Kings, and on the other side of the river are the Karnak and Luxor temples. This is the only one far enough away."

"But how could the game know about Aunt Jillian's tomb?" Amy said.

"Mum's published a book about her findings," Harry told them. "People know about it."

He moved the flashing X at the corner of the screen and set it over the tomb his mother had discovered.

Names appeared on the screen. LUXOR. VALLEY OF THE KINGS. TOMB OF HERI-HOR.

Now the screen flashed, there was a burst of music and words appeared.

"Listen to this." Harry read aloud.

"*Congratulations. Congratulations. You have found the tomb of the forgotten pharaoh Heri-hor. Well played. For your reward, there is a fun game to follow.*

"I don't understand." Harry blinked at the game. "Where's the treasure? It's led us to an empty tomb."

"What else can you expect from a game? Switch the dumb thing off," Josh said disgustedly.

But Harry wanted to keep going.

"Not yet, Josh. Let's just see what's next," he said.

A new game called Secret Touch-stones came up on the screen. Harry pressed the start button.

This time the archaeologist in the game found himself trapped inside a sealed chamber. He had to find his way out by locating a secret stone in the wall and pressing it to activate a lever. Harry moved the X on the screen on to a block of stone and pressed the fire button. Wrong! A trapdoor opened, almost swallowing the archaeologist. Harry made him jump. He chose another stone, pushed the button. A stone in the floor slid open. Quickly, Harry jabbed the button to leap aside.

"Almost got me that time!"

Again he chose a stone and jabbed. Success! A hidden door slid open to reveal a secret passage. Harry sent his character racing through to the next chamber.

"This is good," he said.

Josh left them and went out on deck.

What an idiot I've been to believe a game could lead us to a tomb, he thought. Why did I allow myself to be sucked in?

And yet it *had* seemed to be leading somewhere.

The words of the shop attendant and his son echoed

ironically in his ears now.

"*What do we find at the end?*" Harry had asked.

"*A surprise,*" the Egyptian boy had replied with an unpleasant smile.

It was a surprise all right. Nothing. An empty tomb.

"*Be warned,*" the man had said. "*The Mummy Tomb Hunt is not easy. There are difficult puzzles, dangerous tomb traps ... if you get that far.*"

There had been tomb traps ... but only in silly cartoon games.

I should have left computer games alone, Josh thought bitterly.

And yet ...

It wasn't just the game that had given them clues. There had been other clues, other echoes, real-life ones.

If only he could put the pieces together.

Maybe the game couldn't lead them to an undiscovered tomb, even though it seemed to be helping them: but maybe, just maybe, if they used their brainpower—and their knowledge—they could find something themselves.

The game had let them down. But maybe knowledge and brainpower wouldn't.

He decided to go back to the library.

"That's something I never thought I'd see," Amy said, coming into the library with Harry behind her. "Josh, this isn't school. You're not supposed to be knocking yourself out studying books. You're on holiday. You said the library wasn't for you, remember?"

Josh grinned. "That was a few days ago. I'm looking

for something now, but I don't know what. We have all the pieces of the puzzle, but we need some glue to stick them together." There was an untidy pile of books at his elbow, and he had spread out all the riddles across the table like a paperchase. He selected the very first clue.

"Do you remember Philae?" He read it out. "*Try to find the place where the priests have left no trace, no footprints on the floor, no goddess to adore.* That linked up with Aunt Jillian's discovery in the tomb of the architect Setekhy. Do you remember Setekhy's boast?"

Amy nodded. "Yes. He said something about supervising the journey of the king's coffin to Abydos so that the king could visit the Staircase of the God Osiris—the ladder to heaven—before returning for the burial in the Valley of the Kings. And he said that he did all this like a priest leaving a shrine, going backwards and wiping the ground with palm leaves to hide his footsteps."

"Then there was this clue, which is supposed to be a key to the whole mystery." Josh picked up another piece of paper. "*Sail like a mummy on its pilgrimage cruise, but was it a visit—or merely a ruse?* That seemed to say Heri-hor and his architect were up to something," he added. "So maybe Abydos is where he was buried after all. Setekhy didn't take the pharaoh's body back to the Valley of the Kings, but had it buried secretly at Abydos. The sneaky architect could have gone back to Thebes on board a funerary boat with an empty sarcophagus, disguising his actions—like a priest backing out of a shrine and wiping away the traces of his footsteps."

"It could all have been a big lie to hide the true

resting place of his master," Amy said. "Clever Setekhy."

"Clever *us* for tracking down Heri-hor this far," Harry said.

"But there's one thing I can't understand," Josh said. "Aunt Jillian said she searched the royal cemetery area high and low without finding anything. And why was there no record of Heri-hor being buried there? How could a pharaoh have been buried secretly in Egypt's busiest pilgrimage site?"

"He must have been buried in a place where nobody could see," Harry said, stating the obvious.

Josh read the last riddle.

"There are crooked steps that you must follow,
or your quest for me will turn out hollow.
To the underworld up in the air
take the journey, for my tomb is there."

"How come the game ended up at Aunt Jillian's tomb?" Amy asked.

"That's easy," Harry said. "Mum's discoveries are well known. That tomb is one of the most recent finds in the Valley of the Kings." He sighed. "The thing I can't forget is what the man in the games shop said. He promised it would lead to a *real* forgotten pharaoh's tomb."

"He didn't, he only hinted at it," Amy corrected him.

"Yes, but he did seem to know something," Josh argued. He conjured up a mental picture of the man with the hooked nose. No sooner had the image appeared than another jumped into his mind, taking its place. It was the snarling figure of the animal-headed god Seth, standing in the shop window.

"I never said this before," Amy confessed, " but I always thought it was a bit creepy having a game lead us step by step to a real tomb. Why would a game do that?"

"You tell me," said Josh.

11

Fragments

When the boat reached Nag Hamadi, some distance from Abydos, Aunt Jillian gave the children another choice.

"I want you to decide," she said. "You can join the other passengers on a trip to the temples of Seti and Rameses, or come with me on a visit to the cenotaph temple of king Heri-hor."

Their replies hit her with the force of a gale and made her blink in surprise.

"We're coming with you!" they said in unison.

"Well, just as long as you've made up your minds ..."

The archaeologist Amira, who had joined them at Luxor, had driven on to Nag Hamadi to meet them there. While the other passengers boarded coaches for a visit to the temples of Abydos, they climbed into his four-wheel-drive vehicle and headed off on a forty-minute drive to Aunt Jillian's site. It lay in the desert, beyond the green strip of cultivation.

A great deal of restoration had taken place, Josh observed, comparing the site with his recollections of the slides Aunt Jillian had shown. Columns had been erected and stone walls rebuilt.

Aunt Jillian and Amira inspected the restorations and, in between inspections, Aunt Jillian showed the children around the site. She told them how she had found the first stone under the sand, and described the patient work involved in uncovering the rest, season after season. They went through courtyards, vestibules and chambers, saw the remains of an ancient Nilometer, and then went on to visit the sanctuary.

After their tour of inspection, Aunt Jillian and Amira went off to discuss plans for the next season and the three children found a cool spot in the shade of a temple wall where they sat down to think.

Fragments, memories of words and images, were trying to fit themselves together in Josh's mind.

He remembered the Nilometer in the temple of Edfu.

Where the temple serpent
spirals down to drink,
remember this clue:
you're on the brink.
Cold as stone,
covered in scale,
press for the secret:
you must not fail.

"He must have been buried in a place where nobody could see," Harry had said later.

A familiar phrase came yet again into Josh's mind: *Staircase of the God.* Pharaohs wanted to be buried near the Staircase of the God.

And then something that seemed irrelevant came back to him. It was one of the play sequences in the game where Harry's archaeologist character was running up and down steps. Steps could go up and steps could go down.

What if the Staircase of the God didn't run *up* like a ladder to heaven, but *down* ... like a serpent spiralling down to drink!

"The Nilometer!" Josh whispered. "Maybe we're not finished after all!"

"You mean there *is* a tomb and it's in the Nilometer here?" Harry said, his eyes widening.

"Is it so crazy?"

Harry turned and ran.

Josh and Amy climbed to their feet and went after him.

Make us right, Josh thought. *Please, please.*

Harry reached the steps of the Nilometer, and waited for his cousins to catch up.

"What are you going to do, Harry?"

"I think the tomb of Heri-hor is down here and I'm going to find it!" Harry looked as if he was going to burst with excitement. "Imagine! The tomb of a pharaoh, just waiting for us!"

"Maybe we should call Aunt Jillian," Amy said, trying to speak in a steady voice.

"First we must find out if we're right," Harry said.

He dug out his torch and went on down the steps. "Come on, you two, hurry up if you're coming," he said. "Before Mum sees what we're doing and tries to stop us."

12

The Staircase of the God

Harry went ahead of the others down the shaft. The stairs spiralled around the walls, down and down, to the bottom of the ancient subterranean Nilometer.

"I hope there isn't a real serpent in this one," Harry said.

"Don't say scary things," Amy said.

"Aren't you scared, Josh?" Harry asked.

"Terrified."

"Of what?"

"Being wrong."

In his mind he heard again Aunt Jillian's voice telling him that people were given skills for a reason—and as long as they used those skills in a good cause, that was all that mattered. His ability at playing computer games meant that he had problem-solving skills.

"*Keep those skills sharp, Josh,*" she had said. "*One day they'll serve you well.*"

Would they? Was he right?

They came to a sheet of still black water.

They had reached the bottom.

And so had Josh. There was nothing down here, just

some old stagnant water. He played his torchlight on the surface. It was murky and resisted the beam.

Nothing. No secret passage. No pharaoh's tomb. Just a dirty old well that had once been a Nilometer and probably no longer connected with the Nile.

"Maybe there's a clue down here somewhere," Harry said hopefully, examining cracks in the stone wall.

"I wish we had a riddle from the game to help us," Amy said.

"We're not going to be given any more," Josh said. "The game's over. It's led us as far as it's going to. From now on, we have to find our own clues."

"Let's go up," Amy said. But Josh still lingered. How could he have thought they would find a tomb that Aunt Jillian had missed? It seemed so unlikely now.

And yet he had been so sure.

"Maybe we should try pressing the right stone," Harry suggested. "Like in Secret Touch-stones."

"That was just a stupid game," Josh said.

"Yes, but it could be a clue," Harry argued. "Remember the other part of the riddle: *Cold as stone, covered in scale, press for the secret: you must not fail.*"

"The scale!" Amy said. "Maybe it's the scale used to measure the height of the water down here." She shone her torchlight on some stones in the wall, illuminating deeply incised measurements. Josh and Harry added their torchlight to hers. "Do you think if we pressed one of those marked stones it might open a secret passage?"

"I'm going to find out," Harry said.

"Don't slip, Harry."

He went down to a lower step.

"I'll try pushing the top one. Watch this." He rested his hands on the stone and shoved.

The stone moved a fraction. He pushed again, and his feet went from under him. Josh and Amy made a grab for him as he tumbled over the edge of the step. He stared down at the black water, wild-eyed, as they hauled him back.

"Thanks, guys."

"Maybe it needs a harder push. Let's do it together."

Putting their hands to the top stone, they pushed as hard as they could.

The staircase turned around them. The sound of stone grinding on stone filled their ears, and then came a flushing sound like a giant cistern emptying, followed by a sucking sound like water draining down a plughole.

Josh turned around and shone his torch at the bottom of the Nilometer.

The water had disappeared, and black, slimy steps led away into the darkness.

Josh gave a yell of triumph that echoed up and down the shaft.

"We did it ourselves!" Amy said in amazement. "We've found our secret passage! What now?"

"I know what I'm going to do," Harry said without hesitation. "I'm going down."

"Nobody knows we're here," Amy said sensibly. "If we got stuck, nobody would ever know what happened to us."

"They'd just come down the stairs."

"Not if the water came back. Who knows how long the water will stay away?"

"We can't stop now," Harry said. "Come on, I'm going."

"Careful, Harry. You've slipped once, and those steps are even more slippery from being under the water," Josh advised him.

"I'll be careful."

"What'll we do, Josh?" Amy said.

"You stay up here. I'll go with Harry. We won't be long."

"And leave me here?"

"It's best. If anything goes wrong, you can call Aunt Jillian."

"All right," she said reluctantly, "but don't be long. And if you see anything fantastic, call me. I don't want to miss out."

The gleaming wet steps corkscrewed down endlessly, it seemed. Josh and Harry went carefully, trying to keep their footing on the slimy stone.

When they reached the bottom, Josh's torchbeam gave a wobble of excitement. The steps didn't end there! There were more steps, this time *going up again!* They paused at the bottom of the well, playing their torches on the new flight of stairs. The walls down here were greasy looking and smelled stale and sour, Josh noted, breathing shallowly.

"Up we go," Harry said, climbing eagerly.

Josh went after him. Harry was soon panting like a steam train with the effort of the climb.

The steps ended at a stone landing. Beyond it lay a

dark passage.

"Josh!"

The funnelled scream was twisted out of shape by the walls of the shaft. They heard running footsteps, and shone their torches down to see Amy's wild, upturned face.

"What is it, Amy?"

"Something ..." She was breathless.

"What?"

"I came a little way down so that I could hear you. Then I saw something."

"Where?"

"Coming down after me."

"What was it?"

"A shadowy thing."

"Just a shadow," Josh said, trying to calm her.

"A shadow with pointy ears?" she said. "You don't believe me!"

He went down the steps to join her.

"You're getting jumpy, Amy! Sorry for leaving you alone."

"Shh—"

Josh listened.

"I saw something. It was moving."

"So was your torchlight, I'll bet!"

"I'm not going back there."

"You must. Somebody should stay outside."

A grating sound rumbled around them, and now they heard an explosion of gushing water.

Josh and Amy raced after Harry. Inky water boiled up the steps behind them.

They were sealed in a trap.

13

Breakthrough!

They stood at the edge of the stone landing, looking down forlornly at the flooded steps.

There was no way back to the surface and no hope that anybody would find them. Aunt Jillian did not know about the secret passage in the Nilometer. Their search for a forgotten tomb had led them to disaster.

"We're trapped!" Amy said. "And there's nothing we can do!"

"Maybe there's another stone lever that'll empty the Nilometer," Josh said.

They searched the stone walls of the landing. Amy found the outline of a jackal-headed man painted on a wall and trained a wavery torchbeam on it. "That's the shadowy thing I thought I saw," she said.

"Wepwawet, the guardian of the Abydos cemeteries," Josh said.

"Never mind that." Harry directed the light of his torch at the passage entrance that went beyond the landing. "I want to know where this leads. Come on, you two. We're not going to find a pharaoh's tomb while we stand around here. Let's go on. We may find another way out."

They followed Harry along the passage. The floor was firm, dry stone. There had been no water here. The passage continued for about twenty metres, then came to what looked like a doorway, but was a blank wall. A dead end.

"Perfect," Josh said flatly.

"Wait, that's not a solid wall," Harry said. "That's a plaster wall. And look, there are official seals stamped on the surface." Harry's torchlight illuminated one of the imprints on the plaster: an oval containing hieroglyphs of nine bound prisoners with a seated jackal above them.

"That's the seal of the Necropolis priests!" Harry exclaimed. "I've seen it before—on my mum's empty tomb in the Valley of the Kings. Do you know what this could mean? We've discovered a sealed, intact tomb!"

The children looked at each other in silent wonder.

Did a great discovery lie beyond this doorway—the sort of discovery every Egyptologist dreams of? The fabulous riches of a long-lost pharaoh?

"Maybe we shouldn't get too excited," Harry said, trying to control the tremor in his voice. "Nearly all the tombs discovered in Egypt have already been disturbed. Even Tutankhamun's tomb was entered by robbers before Howard Carter discovered it, although fortunately not too much damage was done."

"But the seal of the priests—it's still here on the door," Amy said, running her finger over the impression in the plaster. "Doesn't this tell us that the tomb inside is intact?"

Harry shook his head. "The priests could have resealed the door after a break-in. It's happened before. In fact, the same thing happened with Tutankhamun's tomb."

"Let's take a look," Amy said eagerly.

Josh searched around for something he could use to break down the door. In the wall of the passage he noticed a section of stone that had split. He put his fingers into a crack and tugged. A big chunk hit the floor.

Good. The stone had broken into several sharp-ended pieces which could be used like picks. They each grabbed one and set to work, hammering on the plaster.

"Be careful. We mustn't destroy valuable evidence," Harry warned them. "See if you can keep some of these Necropolis seals in one piece. They'll be valuable clues for Mum."

At first the plaster resisted, then a crack appeared and a chunk was dislodged, allowing a draft of air to rush out through the hole, which was at the height of Josh's head.

"That air may be thousands of years old," Harry told them. They all breathed in the odour of centuries.

Josh stood on tiptoe and put his torch to the hole, and the others crowded around him as he peered into the chamber beyond. There was a moment of silence.

"Well?" Harry said.

"What do you see, Josh?" Amy's voice was strained.

"Things. Wonderful things," he breathed. "*Strange animals, statues and gold—everywhere the glint of gold!*"

Amy jumped to see past him.

"Hang on," Harry said. "I've heard those words before. That's what Howard Carter said when he first looked into Tutankhamun's tomb through a hole in a wall. Are you fooling around, Josh?"

"Sorry," Josh confessed with a grin. "Only kidding. You're right: I read it in a book in the cruise boat's library. The truth is, I can't see much at all. Only paintings on the walls of a passage."

"You shouldn't tease, Josh!" Amy said, digging him with her elbow. "You got us all excited."

"Then stay excited, because we're on the edge of something," he promised her. "Something Aunt Jillian knows nothing about. Let's knock down more of this doorway so we can go on."

When the hole was big enough, they squeezed through to the other side and found themselves in a painted passageway.

They shone their torches on richly coloured frescoes. Their amazed eyes fell on scenes of a pharaoh travelling through the underworld in his funerary barque, attended by gods and goddesses. Above him were the threatening coils of the great serpent Apophis.

"I wish I could read hieroglyphics," Harry said. "There's a cartouche on the wall." He pointed it out. "That oval shape that looks like a loop of rope. A cartouche always has a name written inside. I'll bet it says Heri-hor. I'll bet this is the tomb Mum's been looking for!"

"Could it really be?" Amy said in awe. "And we've found it for her!"

Josh felt all the pieces of the puzzle coming together and clicking into place.

But would Aunt Jillian ever know? They might never get out of here to tell her. They were as lost as any forgotten pharaoh.

The silence of this tomb world made Josh's ears buzz. *We may be the first and the last ever to see this place since it was sealed thousands of years ago*, a voice in his mind whispered to him. He decided to ignore the voice. Getting out was another problem. Right now they were going to make a discovery, one that might rival the discovery of the tomb of Tutankhamun.

They followed the passage. At first Josh took the lead, but Harry soon raced past him.

The game returned to Josh's mind—not the hunt for the solution to riddles, but the game sequence where the player had to dodge tomb traps. He recalled the warning of the man in the shop in Cairo:

"The Mummy Tomb Hunt is not easy. There are difficult puzzles, dangerous tomb traps ... if you get that far."

When the passage widened into a gallery with a floor of square flagstones, Josh was startled to see a face peering out of a door. No, not one face, but a row of faces, partly concealed by recessed false doorways. He looked up at the first figure.

"Soul statues," Harry said.

Josh flashed a beam of light at the tan-coloured face, and the eyes, of inlaid obsidian with brilliant white surrounds, fixed him with a paralysing stare. The painted stone figure stood like a guard in a sentry box on a heavy base of stone. Its hands were clenched at its sides and it leaned forward at an aggressive tilt.

Josh stopped. Something about that tilt bothered him.

Harry moved on.

Josh lunged at Harry's shirt, grabbed a fistful of it and yanked, jerking his cousin back. The soul statue on its heavy slab thundered out of its doorway, charged past them with a rush of wind and slammed into the far wall. Harry and Amy screamed. The floor trembled.

Harry, who had dropped his torch in fright, picked it up gingerly with an outstretched hand, not daring to step on another flagstone.

"Are you all right, Harry?"

"I think so."

"It must have been set on rollers," Josh said, "triggered when you stepped on a stone. It's my guess the other statues will also be set to go off."

They stood close together, not daring to move on.

To go through the gallery they would have to run a gauntlet of soul statues standing on slabs—ancient man-shaped missiles from the past, loaded and set to punish those who violated the tomb.

"What do we do now?" Harry asked forlornly.

"I don't see how we can go on," Amy said.

"Unless ..." Josh murmured to himself.

14

Running the Gauntlet

Josh was thinking about the tomb trap game again. He remembered the play sequence where blocks of stone kept falling out of the ceiling, threatening to squash the little archaeologist hero on the display.

Speed. That had been the only way to avoid the falling blocks then.

Maybe it was the secret here too.

"If you walked in front of one of those statues, you'd be squashed flat for sure. But what if you ran? I mean *really* ran, sprinted at full speed, as if you were doing the hundred metres dash? I'm going to try it. I'll run Herihor's gauntlet. I'll be too quick for them, and the statues will fly out harmlessly behind me. That way it'll be safe for you two to follow later."

"You're going on your own?"

"You're not fast enough."

"I came second in the girls' fifty metres race at our school," Amy reminded him.

"I know you did. But we need our best speed to get past safely."

"You could be squashed by one of those things," Amy said. "I won't let you do it."

"We don't have a choice. We have to go on. Another way out may lie ahead. And I want to see Mr Heri-hor's tomb even more now. He must have had something to hide!"

"Good luck, Josh," Harry said. "You can beat them!"

"Shine your torches ahead so I can see where I'm going," Josh told them. He dropped into the sprint position like a runner on the starting-block, his torch held like a relay baton.

"Count me down."

"I will!" Harry said eagerly. "Ready? Ten, nine, eight, seven …"

Josh suddenly wished he had his skateboard here. He could whisk along so fast he'd make those stone heads spin.

"Six, five, four, three. …"

Josh tensed. *Don't think about those statues waiting to shoot out and crush you …*

"Two, one … *Go, Josh!*"

But he did think of those statues, and fear set off the muscles in his legs like springs, sending him flying into the gallery.

Whoomph!

It was like stepping on a trigger. The gallery rumbled and a black wind ripped behind him.

Build up speed. Keep low. He was running into blackness. The seeking torchbeams behind him grew fainter. *What if there's something else up ahead, waiting? Another trap. A pit …*

Don't think of that. It'll slow you. Just pump those legs and arms, and fly like a shadow.

Ker-runch!

Another soul statue charged.

He glimpsed the whites of inlaid eyes looming over him as he flicked past. *Crash!* The painted stone attacker slammed into the opposite wall. It was working. The statues were designed to trap tomb-robbers, those proceeding cautiously along the gallery, fearful of what might lie ahead, not a boy running at full stretch in a good pair of sneakers.

Boom!

Another soul statue tried to carry him off into eternity, but Josh was past.

Am I through?

He turned his head to look. It cost him speed. Another soul statue hurtled out of its doorway.

Josh tried to jump clear and tripped on an uneven flagstone. He spun and fell. The statue hit the wall, throwing up a shower of sparks. But he was still alive, and the torch was still in his hand.

"Josh!" Amy's voice echoed from the far end of the gallery. "Are you all right?"

Josh tried to get up. Something pulled at his leg. Puzzled, he shone his torch down. The slab had pinned the bottom of his jeans and the shoelace of his sneaker. He hauled more vigorously. No good. He was stuck.

"We're coming!"

Amy and Harry took off from the far end. Josh could do nothing but shine his torch on the floor to light their way.

Whoomph!

A soul statue on its slab rumbled out of a doorway and flew at the two running figures.

Oh no! Not all the statues had been discharged!

He saw horror on the faces of Harry and Amy as the massive figure roared past them.

And now another.

They must have been set to go off in a random order.

"Faster!" Josh yelled.

Amy and Harry bent low, the torchbeams in their flying hands bouncing light off the walls and roof. They were running the race of their lives.

Here came another. It seemed to slide out more quickly than the others—or were Harry and Amy slowing?

They were past, but it had clipped Harry's heel. He fell to the floor.

Amy, just ahead of him, hadn't noticed. Her face was screwed up in her effort to squeeze the last possible bit of speed from her legs.

Another statue rumbled out, shot behind her and cracked against the wall, but Amy was home.

"Amy, I can't get up," Josh yelled. "Help me. I have to get Harry!"

Amy spun around.

"Where is he?" she gasped.

She shone her torch back into the gallery. Harry had climbed to one knee and had frozen in that position, too afraid to move further. He was as rigid as the statue that loomed just ahead of him, waiting to thunder out.

Amy looked at Josh. "I'll get Harry."

"Amy, you can't. You'll never get up enough speed!"

"Watch me," Amy said. Then she called, "Don't you move, Harry!"

It was a needless warning. Harry was still playing statues on the floor, and his eyes were showing more of their whites than the eyes of the soul statue. The man-missile had hypnotised him.

Amy took off.

Josh had missed the race at school where Amy had come in second. He wished he'd seen it now. He'd been surprised by her final burst of speed down the gallery when Harry had taken his tumble. But speed driven by fear was one thing, and speed driven by the urge to protect another human being was another.

Amy flew down the corridor.

"Go, Amy!" Josh shouted.

Whoomph!

A soul statue went by on its block like a runaway truck.

Missed her.

She'd get to Harry, but to pick him up she would have to lose momentum. Could she build up enough speed to get back?

Josh stared along his torchbeam. The soul statue in front of Harry waited, tilted forward, begging for its chance.

Harry saw Amy reaching out for him. He put out his hand, but his knees were locked in fright.

Amy grabbed his wrist and catapulted Harry to his feet. The waiting soul statue gave a ghastly wobble on its rollers as if nodding its head, and then it ground out swiftly to attack.

Amy dived with Harry. They both did a tumble. The

shuddering figure screeched across the floor.

Bang! It hit the wall.

Back on their feet, Amy and Harry leaned forward in a dash to capture speed. Amy still had Harry by the wrist, and his feet almost flew above the floor.

Another statue shot out. Amy had hit full pace. She towed Harry out of the last few metres of the gauntlet.

They were home safely.

She collapsed on the floor on her back, wheezing, dragging air into her lungs.

Harry gave a frightened giggle.

"That was fun," he said between gasps.

Together, Amy and Harry managed to rip the bottom of Josh's jeans and the shoelace free from the slab that pinned them down.

They went on through the gallery, which throttled down to a narrow passage.

"Thanks, Amy," Harry said in a small voice, when he had recovered his composure. "I'm sorry. I couldn't move. You were fantastic. You saved me."

Amy shrugged. "I did it without thinking."

"Without thinking of yourself, you mean. I never thought I'd see my sister try such a brave stunt," Josh said teasingly. "Aunt Jillian would be proud of you."

Josh marvelled at how just a few days in Egypt had changed their lives. He had found a new interest, and, with the help of the game and the others, maybe even a tomb. Amy had found something just as precious: her courage.

The passage climbed to a lofty gallery level.

"Stop!"

Josh's torchbeam, travelling along the floor, was suddenly sucked into an abyss.

They stopped in a line, teetering on an edge, their toes jutting over a black shaft that fell into nothingness.

A tomb pit.

15

Tomb Pit

A length of halfa grass rope trailed over the edge of the pit and snaked down into the blackness—the first sign that others had been this way before. It was attached to a spur of rock in the wall. The children searched the far side, hoping to find another rope leading out of the pit.

"What'll we do now?"

"What the tomb-robbers did," Josh said, guessing. "They may have thought this pit led down to treasure. I wonder why they didn't come up the other side?"

"How could they reach it?"

"By using a grappling hook on the end of a rope," Josh said. "They could swing it up from down there."

"Maybe they didn't have one," Harry said.

"Then why did they leave their rope here when they climbed back up?"

"Who said they climbed back up?" Harry suggested darkly. "Maybe they're still down there … or what's left of them."

"If they went down a rope, they could just as easily come up again," Amy pointed out.

"Not if something got them."

"Don't be silly, Harry. But I'd like to know how they got into this section. We didn't see any sign of entry to the tomb. And they obviously didn't disturb those mad statues back there."

"Maybe they tunnelled in somewhere and the tunnel's been filled in. The priests could have discovered it and resealed it later," Josh said. "I'll go down.

"I'll go, if you like," Amy said. "After dodging those flying statues, climbing down a rope seems pretty tame."

"Yesterday you were amazed that Aunt Jillian could abseil down a cliffside."

"That was yesterday."

"No, you've taken enough chances," Josh said. "I'll go down first."

He bent and tested the rope, feeling the rough fibre between his fingers. It seemed strong enough. He wondered how long ago the tomb-robbers had used it.

Pocketing his torch, he took hold of the rope and went over the edge of the tomb pit.

"Shine your lights down here so I can see where I'm going," he called.

He lowered himself gingerly, hand over hand. Bumping and scraping against the wall, he dropped lower and lower, using the rubber soles of his sneakers to brake himself. He remembered what Aunt Jillian had said about abseiling down a cliff. *"It was easy. What's more scary is going down a tomb pit when you can't even see the bottom."*

He dared to look down.

No glint of water. But there were shapes down there.

He was near the bottom when he took another look. The glow from the two torches above trickled down faintly, like starlight. It revealed the shapes of bones—human bones, he guessed—and something else: the skeletons of long creatures with tails and stubby legs. Crocodiles?

He reached the end of the rope and dropped the short distance to the bottom. Bones crunched under his feet. He dug his torch out of his pocket and shone it around.

"Okay, Josh?" Amy called down.

"All okay."

Near the bones lay a coil of rope. He tested it between his fingers. It was strong and dry. There had been no water down here recently or it would have rotted.

His torchlight illuminated the other bones. Where had the crocodiles come from? He shone his light down the length of the pit. He could see what might once have been an opening but was now almost hidden, collapsed under tonnes of stone. Maybe an earthquake had trapped the crocodiles here.

It was easy to guess what had happened to the men. The crocodiles had probably been starving. He looked around, squeamishly picking over the skeletons with the toe of his sneaker. And there he found what he was looking for—a metal grappling hook.

"Do you want to go down first, Harry?" Amy asked him.

Josh had thrown up the rope with the grapple lashed to one end, and after several attempts he'd managed to lock it onto the far edge of the pit. He'd hauled himself gratefully to the top.

"What's down there?" Harry called to him across the chasm.

"Just some old bones."

"Bones of what?"

"Tomb-robbers, I'd say. And some other stuff."

"What stuff?"

"Crocodiles."

"Crocodiles!"

"They're dead, Harry."

"You go first, Amy," Harry decided.

"Okay."

"But that would leave me to go last." Uneasiness crept into his voice. "What if the rope broke and I got stuck down there?"

"Then you go first."

"No, maybe you should."

"Are you scared? It's all right to be scared, Harry," she said gently. "I was scared in that passage with those statues, I can tell you."

"Were you? Well, so was I, a bit," Harry confessed. "What should I do, Amy?"

"Go down first, Harry. That way you'll have one of us to help at each end."

"All right."

When they had all crossed safely, Josh coiled the rope and left it at the edge, and they continued their exploration.

After walking through a length of bare stone corridor, the children reached a stretch where the walls on either side were dominated by two enormous painted black jackals. As they approached the paintings, they heard a click, like a spring being released.

Harry saw it first and yelled.

They shrank back.

A towering jackal-headed man slid out of a side passage and spun in front of them, brandishing a war axe and a wickedly curved sword.

Josh felt his heart give a kick under his ribs. He thought at first that the creature was alive. And then he saw the metallic shine of its skin. The head was painted black. The eyes, swept up dramatically in the Egyptian way, were inlaid with shining stones.

It was a mechanical monster, a whirling idol with weapons: Wepwawet, guardian of the tombs of Abydos.

They fell back further and it stopped spinning.

"Look at the floor," Amy said, shuddering.

Two headless skeletons lay at the monster's feet.

16

Wepwawet

They were safe here in the passage for the time being, Josh decided. The mechanical guardian couldn't come any closer. It ran from its hidden recess on some kind of track.

"It can't get to us," he said to the others, reassuringly. "It can't move past that spot where it's standing."

"And neither can we," Harry said, losing some of his usual optimism.

Josh tried to calm his jangled nerves to think.

"There must be a way."

"I wouldn't try sprinting past this one!" Harry advised him. "Unless you want to be sliced salami."

"It looks alive!" Amy said. "Look how its eyes are burning."

"It's mechanical," Josh murmured, more to himself than to the others. *Mechanical.* Think mechanically, he told himself. Use that against it.

"It must be set off when someone treads on the stones on the floor," Harry said.

Josh nodded. "Has to be." He moved as near as he dared and put out a foot to tap the floor. The jackal warrior slashed the air, spinning like a top.

"Good," Josh said. "It did the same thing in the same way."

"What are you planning to do?"

"Stay here. I'm going to get something. I'll only be a moment."

He left, and returned with the coil of rope.

"You're going to tie him up?" Harry said. "Good idea."

"Not so good," Amy said. "He'd slice through the rope."

"I'm going to try something else. But first, Amy, I want you to get Wepwawet into a bit of a spin for me. Press the floor with your foot when I say so."

Josh took the weighted end of the rope, the end with the grapple, and spun it like a lariat. There was just enough room in the corridor for him to give it a good swing. He stood in front of the statue and took aim, not at the head or the body, but at the ankles.

"You're going to pull him off his feet?"

"No, I'm going to let him do the work. There's a powerful mechanism underneath his feet. Now, Amy!"

Josh bent and flicked the grapple down the passage. It flew, the rope streaming behind it, just as Amy pressed the floor with her foot. The statue kicked and spun. The grapple had gone past it. Josh pulled on the rope. The spinning ankles met the grapple and took up a few coils of the rope.

"Lift your foot off!" Josh shouted to Amy. "I need to secure the end of the rope to something."

Amy drew back, but the figure of Wepwawet kept on spinning, and Amy and Harry watched in horror as Josh stumbled towards the spinning blades. With a final squeaky turn, the guardian stopped, facing them.

Josh found a small pillar of stone near the wall. Quickly he lashed the end of the rope to it.

"Got you!" he said to the towering creature.

With a smile on his face, he put out a foot.

Wepwawet spun at once, drawing the rope tight with a twang. The fibres of halfa grass creaked, but did not break. Relentlessly, like a winch, the figure turned. *Creak, creak.* The rope ached. Wepwawet gave a metallic squeal. It began to lean. The turning axe in its metal arm struck a wall. Another few turns and it would topple off its base. But before that happened, Josh's plan came undone. The monster, now bending lower than before, sliced neatly through the rope.

Crack! The broken rope snapped back against a wall.

Wepwawet went into a dizzying spin. But it had lost its centre of gravity and was wobbling on its base. The wobble grew wider and wider and more violent. Then, with a scream of shearing metal, the jackal guardian came off its base and flew into the wall, its flying axe and sword hitting sparks off the stone.

Harry whooped.

The broken giant lay in the passage, its hot metal limbs ticking, splitting little cracks in the silence that now again closed in around them.

"Teach you to mess around with us," Harry told it as they walked past.

More passages, separated by doorways, led to an antechamber. Inside it was a jumbled mess. Statues and piles of boxes were all scattered about as if someone had gone on a rampage.

Harry groaned at the sight. "Tomb-robbers," he said with certainty. "They've been here. I know the signs."

"After all this!" Amy said, her shoulders drooping.

"It depends how far they got with their work. If the priests re-sealed the doorway, maybe they caught them or interrupted them before they could take everything. But how did the robbers get past all the tomb traps? There must be some other tunnel."

Walking on through the antechamber, they came to an empty room with four columns cut out of the stone. They passed through two more corridors, going ever deeper into the tomb, until at last they came to the tomb chamber itself.

"Look out!"

Their torchbeams illuminated the white, inlaid eyes of a pair of black guardians who stood on either side of the door, their golden staves held out in front of them. They weren't the statues of a boy king like Tutankhamun, but had the powerful shoulders and mature features of a man with a warlike face and a curved nose.

"Heri-hor, I'll bet!" Harry exclaimed. "It's the same guy who attacked us in the gauntlet of statues. And these statues are still standing. That's a good sign!"

They passed warily between the stern black sentinels.

But their hopes fell again at the sight of the jumble of grave goods lying on the floor of the burial chamber. Boxes were thrown open. A black jackal decorated with gold leaf had been tipped on its side along with inlaid tables, chairs and couches and a broken golden chariot. A model of a wooden funerary boat, about the size of a canoe, lay in splinters on the floor, its oars, no bigger than paddles, scattered about it.

A vast mummy case covered in a sheet of finely beaten silver metal lay on the floor, its lid pulled aside. They drew nearer and shone their torches inside, expecting to see a mummy, but it was empty.

"How could a mummy have fitted in there ... unless it was a giant," Amy breathed. "It's huge."

"It's an outer coffin, the sarcophagus," Harry said. "The pharaohs' mummies were laid in nests of coffins. The precious ones were in the middle. Don't give up hope yet."

They went around the coffin and through the scattered grave furnishings to the back of the tomb. There stood a shrine, like a giant wardrobe, covered with fine gold leaf. The doors were flung open.

17

Sealed Fate

"There's something inside!" Harry said breathlessly.

They all drew nearer and shone their torches into the shrine. Inside it they could see the base of a shiny metal anthropoid coffin, its feet covered in sandal-shaped designs.

"Oh wow!" Harry said. "Look what we've discovered! This is absolutely brilliant!"

"A pharaoh!" Amy whispered.

Josh gulped as he stared at the case. "Do you think it's gold?"

"No, it's something rarer to the ancient Egyptians and something they thought was much more valuable," Harry said in a torrent of excitement. "Electrum. A mixture of silver and gold. Hundreds of kilos of it! The priests must have caught the robbers before they could take the inner coffin. I suppose it was the priests who shoved this coffin back into the shrine before they sealed up the entrance."

"You'd think they could have tidied up for poor king Heri-hor," Amy said. "What a mess they left in here."

"Maybe they were in a hurry," Josh said. He felt dazed. We've actually done it, he thought exultantly. We've solved the riddle, cracked the mystery.

Inside this intact coffin would be the mummy of the long-dead pharaoh Heri-hor.

Everything made sense now. He remembered what the guide had told them about Edfu, how the Nilometer had once linked up with the Nile and given the priests a secret passage to the river. It was the same thing here. The king had been carried to this tomb on a boat along an underground channel from the river, *none other seeing and none other knowing*. That explained it. It had all been done in secret, below ground.

But what if, having made this discovery, they were never able to tell anybody about it! It was an unbearable thought.

We can't die here! Josh thought. *We must get back.*

"We've got to find a way out," he said. "We've got to find a way to tell Aunt Jillian about this."

"There's no way out," said Amy. "The Nilometer back there is filled with water. You saw it."

"She's right," Harry said, slumping.

They sat on some upturned chests to rest and to think.

"I can't believe we've done all this for nothing!" Amy said in anguish. "If we just sit here the air will run out."

"That could take a long time," Josh said. "There's a whole length of passage out there going all the way back to the flooded steps."

"If we're stuck here and die," Harry said, his voice wobbling, "it won't have been such a great adventure."

"More like a trap," Josh said. "And we've been led into it step by step."

"By the game?" Amy said. "But the game only led us as far as the Valley of the Kings, and an empty tomb."

"I suppose you're right," Josh said. "It's just a doubt I have. The game put the Nilometer idea in our heads. And other things led us on. Do you remember how, in the Mummy Monster Game, Seth tampered with the program to spite us? I haven't been able to get that character out of my head. The man in the shop reminded me of him, and I keep seeing his face. Do you remember how angry he was when we beat him in the Mummy Monster Game?"

"Seth," Harry said, nodding. "The evil brother of Osiris! I wouldn't put it past him. You think he infiltrated the game to get back at us! Do you think he was behind it all along?"

"Who knows?" said Josh. "Maybe we'll never know. But I know one thing for sure. We got here by relying on our brainpower, and not just on the clues of that game. Brainpower is the thing that will save us."

"So it won't all end here," Harry said.

"It won't end here," Josh reassured him. "And I don't think the tomb ends here, either. If my hunch is right, it leads on to the river."

"Where do we look?" Amy said hopefully.

"Behind the shrine is my guess," Josh said.

They squeezed past the shrine and shone their torches on the wall. The light flared on the white plaster of a sealed doorway.

18

Amy

"Good one, Josh!" Harry said. "We're not finished yet."

They went back into the burial chamber to find tools to break the plaster. Josh chose a war axe, Harry chose a royal mace and Amy took one of the wooden paddles they had seen earlier.

They made a small hole in the wall and widened it. A cool, damp-smelling breeze blew in.

"Water. There's water beyond this tomb. Maybe it's the river!"

They cleared more of the wall. Chunks of plaster came crashing down until at last the hole was big enough for them to climb through.

On the other side of the wall, a flight of steps fell away.

Josh went down first. His torchbeam found an answering gleam, the light flaring on a sheet of still green water. He gasped at what he saw gathered around its edge—a horde of ancient Egyptian gods, goddesses and demons.

It wasn't the river. It was a channel that ran through a painted, barrel-vaulted passage. The ceiling and walls were covered with vivid paintings of the Egyptian underworld:

men and women with beetle heads, snake and crocodile heads, jackal heads, cow and ape heads, with eyes like black suns in their brilliant white orbits. They held swords, spears and clubs in their hands. The standing figures on the walls were half submerged by the water.

"We'll have to try swimming for it," Josh said.

"I don't think so," Harry said, shining his torch downwards. "Look."

Something was moving beneath the dark water, a long twisting shape that undulated to propel itself. Josh saw a coil rise towards the surface, and watched the scaly patchwork of a reptile's skin sharpen into focus.

"A snake." He jumped back. "A huge one."

"Maybe it's the monster Apophis, the one who attacked the pharaoh's boat on his journey through the underworld," Harry said, only half-joking. "Do you think it could really live down here?"

"No, I don't. That snake looked pretty real to me. And I think I can see more," Josh said with despair. "Yes, look out there."

They followed the sweep of his torchbeam. Swimming snakes made lethal cross currents on the surface of the channel.

"That means there's no way forward and no way backwards. We really are stuck."

"No we're not," Amy said confidently.

"What do you mean?" Josh said. "Are you going to suggest we try swimming with those things in the water?"

"We don't have to." She waved her paddle in the air. "Playing all these games has made me start to think like a gameplayer. I have a solution. We'll paddle out."

"In what?" Josh said, tiredly. She'd raised their hopes, but she really had no solution at all. "We don't have a boat, Amy."

"No," she said, "but we do have a *big* wooden mummy case. We'll use it as a canoe. It's big enough to fit all of us."

"I wish I'd thought of that!" Josh said. "Brilliant, Sis."

"I wish I'd thought of it, too," Harry said enviously. "Well done, Amy."

Before they could get the big coffin case through the hole in the wall, they had to move the shrine. They found some more lengths of grass rope which they tied around the handles of the shrine, and together they hauled it out far enough to give themselves room to pass the coffin case through.

Josh grabbed a handful of rings from an ornamental inlaid box. "We'll need some proof if we're going to convince Aunt Jillian," he said, pocketing them.

They gathered around the wooden mummy case to carry it out. Heaving and grunting, they hauled it out of the burial chamber and then, bumping, down the steps to the water's edge.

"That metal covering should make it watertight," Josh said. "What do you suppose it is? A sheet of electrum?"

"Looks like it," Harry said.

Amy ran back to the tomb chamber and returned with a paddle for each of them. The paddles had tips like spears and were painted with lotus flower patterns.

They edged the sarcophagus canoe out into the water. It floated. Josh held it steady while the others jumped in, then climbed in after them. Harry sat at the head of the empty mummy case, Amy in the middle and Josh near the feet. Josh pushed away from the steps with the tip of his paddle and they were adrift. The barrel-vaulted ceiling arched over their heads.

Josh looked at the bottom of the mummy case for any sign of a leak. Their flat-bottomed boat seemed to be watertight and remarkably stable. He tried not to think about the snakes in the water.

"Unreal!" Harry yelled in his excitement. "This is better than going on a ghost train ride!"

His voice echoed down the channel, unnaturally loud. The painted eyes of the creatures on the walls seemed to widen.

Josh winced. "Sh-sh. Keep it down, Harry. Now, let's get moving. Two of us will row while one shines a torch ahead."

Harry wanted to row first, so Amy agreed to provide the light with her torch. Josh and Harry dipped their paddle blades into the water and began to propel the strange boat forward.

"Here we go paddling along in our mummy case canoe!" Harry cheered. "I'll bet nobody's ever done this before! I'll bet old Heri-hor never dreamed that his mummy case would one day be a boat, floating through the underworld. I wonder where it's going to take us?"

"Not so noisy, Harry."

Were those ripples spreading from their bow, or the streaming bodies of snakes?

They settled into a steady rhythm, their paddles splashing softly. Amy played her torchbeam on the painted roof of the passage and then down into the water to check for the approach of the giant snake.

"I hope that big snake wouldn't attack a boat," she said.

"That's exactly what Apophis would do," Harry said, shuddering.

"It's just a snake, Harry," Josh said. "It's probably blind from never having seen the light."

"I hope so." Harry took comfort from Josh's words. "And if it isn't blind, it'll probably be frightened by the images on the sides of the coffin. Especially the scary Horus eyes."

When Harry grew tired, Amy took over the paddling and worked strenuously along with Josh.

Harry was fascinated by the pictures of the fierce tomb monsters on the roof and walls of the channel. "These creatures seem to move in the torchlight," he said, wonderingly. "Have you noticed?" He gave a violent jump that made their coffin canoe rock dangerously.

"What are you doing, Harry?"

"It moved."

"You'll turn us over, Harry. You're seeing things. Keep your torch on the water—you'll scare yourself to death."

Harry swung his torch at the wall as a painted baboon-headed monster raised a spear above its head.

"Wow! It's like an Egyptian graphics attack in a game!" Harry said. "Keep paddling!"

19

Voyage through the Underworld

Josh and Amy paddled as hard as they could.

Now an eagle-headed graphic appeared, swinging at them with a curved sword. At the same moment two painted attackers, one on each side of the channel, raised their swords to strike: goddesses with lioness heads and yellow, angry slashes for eyes. Their mouths were open in silent roars of rage.

On the ceiling a vulture-headed woman hovered over them, her great wings outspread, her talons lowered. Harry shone his torchbeam up and saw the wicked curve of claws and beak and the scrawny stretch of a vulture neck.

The bird sailed overhead like a shadow and slid out of sight.

Now Harry's torchbeam fixed on a squat, diamond-shaped head as it reared out of the water.

"Watch out!"

Josh raised his paddle like a spear.

The serpent launched itself at them, its great pink mouth opening. The force of its strike made the boat rock dangerously.

Harry yelled. Amy's eyes were wide with terror as she continued to paddle.

Josh stabbed the pointed blade of his paddle into the snake's mouth. It recoiled, and went down and under the boat. Would it turn them over? One flick of its coils could upset them. It came up on the other side, lifting its head to watch them. Its eyes glowed opaquely like lights in alabaster lamps.

Again it rolled to approach the boat, darting forward like a battering-ram. Josh whacked it on the head, hard. Once more it disappeared under the boat.

Two human-headed birds painted on the ceiling swooped overhead.

The boat rounded a bend in the channel and drifted into a cavern with a high roof. It was an underground lake. There was no exit from the lake except through a small opening on the far side, and a finely meshed bronze gate ending in spikes was rumbling down to meet the water and seal it off. What had activated it? Yet another hidden lever, thought Josh despairingly.

"Paddle faster, Amy!" he yelled. "Keep your light on that gate, Harry!"

Josh and Amy dug deep with their paddles and pulled hard. The exit from the cavern was several metres away, and already the spikes were perilously low.

Not after all this, Josh thought angrily. Not after we've come so far! He looked around. The serpent was close behind them, rearing again to strike the boat.

Josh's body shook with determination. He gritted his teeth and stabbed the blade of his paddle into the water.

He pulled, raised it and plunged again, every sinew and muscle tearing with the effort.

"Faster!" Amy said. "We're not going to get through!"

The spikes of the gate were coming down like teeth. The head of the mummy boat slipped underneath.

"Duck!"

They flung themselves down. The boat began to pass beneath the gate. Josh saw the spikes gouge the air over their heads. *We're going to make it!* Then there was a jarring thump and a squeal of twisting timber, and the boat was almost ripped apart.

They sat up. The spikes had jammed at the foot of the mummy case, stopping it dead.

Could they jump out and swim?

What if there were more snakes?

"Everybody—get to the back!"

Josh, Harry and Amy rolled.

Their combined weight at the foot of the mummy case took it down, dangerously down. It was almost clear, but one spike still held them. Josh grabbed the spike and the back of the boat and shoved them apart, trying to unhook them.

"Lean back a bit more!"

They did, and suddenly they were free.

They scrambled back into the middle of the boat. The gate slid down behind them, sealing the exit, and as it did so, the squat head of the serpent slammed into the mesh.

"He can't get through. We're safe!" Harry cheered.

They were out of the channel and floating on a broad

expanse of river in darkness. They had found an outlet into the Nile.

Later, a fisherman in a felucca dragged them, shivering, on board his boat. He took them back to their cruise boat at Nag Hamadi and somebody went to fetch Aunt Jillian from her site beyond Abydos, where the search for the children was still going on.

Aunt Jillian had been frantic with worry, and it was a while before she managed to control her delight and relief at finding the children safe. When she was calmer, a new shock awaited her.

"We've found your tomb!" said Harry.

"Which tomb?"

"The forgotten pharaoh's tomb!" said Amy.

Josh handed her the evidence of their astonishing find, the golden rings that he had taken from the tomb. She blinked at them, then closed her fingers around them tightly, as though afraid that they would vanish. Almost fearfully, she opened her hand again and gazed at the rings, before looking at the children.

"These are cartouche rings," she said in her whispery voice. "They contain the name of a pharaoh—Heri-hor. What have you children done? Do you have any idea what this evidence means?"

Her shock deepened when the owner of the felucca showed her the mummy case, which he had also rescued.

"That's our mummy case canoe!" Harry said. "It took us on a fantastic ride. It was like being in a tunnel of horror."

Aunt Jillian bent and ran her fingers over the hieroglyphic inscriptions and decorations that covered the outer metal skin of the wooden coffin. She did this in silence, except for an occasional thoughtful "hm" or "ah", like a doctor examining a patient. Then she gave a final grunt and straightened.

"Tell me everything," she said to the children. "Slowly."

They told her, but not slowly; that was impossible. They told her excitedly, interrupting each other in their eagerness to tell it all.

"Josh worked it out, with a bit of help from me," Harry said generously, when they had finished their story. "And Amy, of course," he added.

"With a *heap* of help from Amy," Josh corrected him. "We wouldn't be here to tell anyone about it if Amy hadn't thought of using the mummy case as a boat."

"Sorry, Amy," Harry said quickly. "You were great."

"So were you, Harry."

Aunt Jillian's startled look faded slowly as they told their amazing story. Now she smiled, and shook her head in wonder. "What a family. Come here, all of you," she said, holding out her arms in a rare display of affection. "I want to hug all three of you at once."

And she did.

20

Mr Aboudy and Son

They stopped outside Magical Isis Games and Novelties in the dingy arcade in Cairo.

Harry pressed his nose to the glass.

"Hey, they've changed the window display," he announced. Josh and Amy looked. He was right. The statue of Seth was gone. "And look!" Harry pointed. "Mr Aboudy is back!"

When they went inside, Mr Aboudy and his young son rushed out from behind the counter and greeted their arrival with loud applause.

"You are famous man Mr Harry," the shop-owner said. He was a huge man and his galabea looked as big as a circus tent.

His son, a round-faced, smiling boy, ran and shook hands with Harry. "We have seen your picture in the newspaper and on television. You are great discoverer like Howard Carter!"

"Thank you, but my cousins did most of the work," Harry said, introducing them. The two Egyptians shook Josh and Amy warmly by the hand.

"You are *all* great discoverers like Howard Carter!" said Mr Aboudy. Then he proudly informed Josh and Amy: "Mr Harry is our favourite customer here."

"We missed seeing you," Harry said. "We came here before our trip, but somebody else served us."

Mr Aboudy's face darkened.

"A most upsetting incident. My cousin Omar was supposed to mind the shop, but he fell mysteriously ill and asked another man to take his place until he could make other arrangements—a stranger he had only known for a matter of days! Unbelievable. We came back to find things changed in our shop, and the man and his son ..." His voice trailed off, and he shrugged. "Gone."

"Did you lose anything?" Harry said.

"Only my confidence in my cousin Omar. Most curious. Most curious."

"So was the game that we bought here," Josh told him. "The Mummy Tomb Hunt."

Mr Aboudy brightened.

"The Mummy Tomb Hunt? You have played this game? Excellent, most diverting. Brand new software. And do you know that the game is based on the discoveries of Mr Harry's famous mother?"

"We found that out," Amy said.

"Do you have any more Egyptian games?" Harry asked.

"No, Harry!" Josh and Amy said at once.

"Not for now," Harry said. "For another time."

Mr Aboudy leaned forward as if to take them into his confidence. "I have a new Egyptian game coming in soon," he said. "A most exciting game. It is played in real time."

"What does that mean?" Amy asked.

Josh explained. "Some computer adventure games are like that. They can take weeks to play. Like the submarine game Hunt for Red October. You have to cross an ocean, watching your fuel tanks and air supply as you go. A friend of mine at school was wrecked off the coast of America after dodging the whole Russian fleet."

"But in this new Egyptian game," Mr Aboudy said, "a woman, an archaeologist, is trapped underground in a tomb that has collapsed around her. Her air will run out in a set number of days. You, the players, must find her before the time runs out. But it is a tomb that no other living person knows about."

"Brilliant!" Josh said.

"I couldn't stand it!" Amy laughed.

"I'll order it," Harry said eagerly. "Send me a copy as soon as it's in, Mr Aboudy!"

Mr Aboudy smiled.

Josh and Amy shook their heads. Harry never tired.

Josh wondered how long it would be before they played the next game from Harry's favourite little games shop in Cairo.

He hoped it wouldn't be *too* long.